Wicked o Past

Paranormal in Manhattan Mystery:

Book 4

By Lotta Smith

Copyright

To hear about new books and discounted book sales, please sign up for my newsletter at:
http://eepurl.com/bOSLYj
And follow me on http://amzn.to/22h0TSf

Prologue: Part I

11:42 p.m., Christmas Eve, Last Year…

She was lying there, motionless. She was so still, to the point of almost looking like a dead body.

It was one of those chilling winter nights in Manhattan where you felt cold to the bone. Laid out cold, she still had feelings…. She could feel her blood draining out of herself.

Oddly, she didn't feel pain. That was truly strange, considering she fell from her balcony on the fifth floor and she had a huge gash in her head.

Am I going to die? she wondered. She was in her condo's perimeter, but she had a hunch that her fellow residents weren't likely to notice her demise anytime soon. Thanks to her still-intact hearing, she could hear people laughing, singing, and having a good time.

Her situation reminded her of the many victims she'd killed off in the past. She let out a low chuckle and grimaced. For the first time, she felt a scathing pain.

The snow flurried over her body.

She wondered whether or not her death was going to be ruled as a suicide…

And if this day was going to be the last for Carina Christien…

Prologue: Part II

Rick Rowling twitched his eyebrows as he felt a jolt of pain in his right leg. Originating from the ankle, the pulsating sensation shot through his lower leg and thigh, followed by a dull heat sweeping up to his buttocks.

Realizing that he'd unwittingly moved his broken ankle while dozing on the sofa, he felt like cursing.

Instead, he lay there unmoving, keeping his eyes tightly shut. Cursing was tempting, but considering he felt like he'd been in a train wreck, it wasn't such a good idea. In an attempt to brush off the pain, he tried to focus on something different, like the ski trip he'd planned recently, but that thought made him even more miserable. According to the doctor, going on a ski trip in his condition, even though it was only a little crack in a small bone, was the silliest idea she'd heard in months.

Wrinkling his nose, Rick wondered what had gotten him into this mess. Though he'd always prided his sharp reflexes, some recklessness and a freak accident were enough to get him hurt. Under normal circumstances, there was no way he'd succumb to such a ridiculous injury as having his leg crushed by a bookcase that was falling very slowly.

Still, I couldn't just run away and watch her

get squashed, he concluded, recalling the incident just hours ago.

When he saw Mandy, his assistant, frozen in place as the bookcase threatened to smash her, he instinctively ran toward the collapsing furniture. Anyone with elementary school-level physics knowledge knew that running toward the falling object—especially a heavy object—was a bad idea, but he dared to do it, and with a full understanding of the consequences.

What was I thinking? Did I have some childish delusion of being Batman or some other superhero with a silly name? He wasn't big about sacrificing himself, but he just couldn't stand the possibility of Mandy being wounded.

Maybe it was the pain meds messing with his head, but he suddenly found a crooked humor in the whole situation. Then he was chuckling like an idiot, which led to immediate regret, another jolt of pain shooting up his leg.

"Shit!" Growling, he stretched an arm, grabbing for the air. He was taken by surprise when another hand took his.

When he opened his eyes, he found Mandy holding his hand in hers, sitting by his side in his living room.

"Rick, are you okay? You've been asleep for about an hour, but you didn't look well for the past couple minutes. Did you have a bad dream or something?" She looked at him with genuine concern in her eyes.

"I'm fine," he mumbled, confused by the sight of her at his home. "Mandy, what are you doing here?"

She furrowed her eyebrows in response and

gave his hand a gentle pat. "I'm staying here with you to help you get around until you heal. By the way, you're the one who came up with this plan, rejecting your doctor's suggestion to arrange a nurse, remember?"

"Oh, now I remember," he whispered softly, recalling the conversation.

"Good." She nodded, releasing her hand from his and gently touching his right shin. "Ooh, look at your leg. It's swollen. Does it hurt?"

"Um… yeah. It's a little bit sore." He let out a sigh, thinking 'a little bit sore' was the understatement of the year. He avoided looking at his bad leg, but assuming from the persistent heat and tightness, it didn't take a rocket scientist to picture an ankle the size of a melon.

"I'll get you some ice to put on it. How does that sound?"

"I like that. Thanks."

"No problem. One moment." Mandy stood up and scurried to the bar counter to fix an ice bag.

Watching her scooping ice cubes into a plastic bag, a smile worked its way across Rick's face.

Maybe it's not as bad as it seemed.

Spending a whole summer recovering from an injury sucked big-time, not to mention his leg was still throbbing like hell. Then again, the prospect of Mandy staying with him and caring for him blew away all the setbacks.

He really, *really* liked the arrangement.

CHAPTER 1

1:34 p.m., December 10th

It started with a phone call.

On a lazy Saturday afternoon, I was at home, sitting on the sofa by the floor-to-ceiling window in the living room, taking in the unobstructed view of Midtown Manhattan and people frolicking to the Christmas tree at Rockefeller Center.

Yes, you heard me right. I could see New York City's most iconic Christmas tree from my living room!

Okay, so technically, it wasn't *my* living room. The lavish condo, including but not limited to the state-of-the-art library and the huge blue marble hot tub, belonged to Rick Rowling, my condo-mate who also happened to be my boss at the FBI's Paranormal Cases Division.

At the moment, he was out and I was pretending to be the queen of the place, admiring the Christmas tree down below and the one in Rick's living room, which we'd recently installed. While trying to figure out what was inside the Christmas gift addressed to me—my guess was a teddy bear, assuming from the shape, though it could've been a rabbit with the ears folded—I was having me-time, reading a hot, steamy romance by Violet Huss, an emerging author whose works started to appear on multiple bestsellers' lists.

In my head, I was picturing Bella, the heroine,

and Henry, the hero—a self-made billionaire CEO who was also a vampire—engaging in kinky sex in the hot tub. As I wondered why it was as easy as eating a cupcake for fictional characters to have sex, and how spanking and drinking each other's bodily fluid—*I mean, yuck!*—had become such a rage nowadays, Jackie popped up from out of nowhere.

"Hey, girlfriend. What's up?"

"I'm good, thanks. How are you?" I smiled nonchalantly but briskly switched off the screen of my Kindle.

"Come on, Mandy. You don't need to hide it from me." Jackie winked. "I love steamy romance books sooo much! And I'll tell you, Violet Huss is my favorite author!" Jackie was in her usual getup of a colorful, skimpy top, but her short skirt had changed its colors into red and white, just like Santa Claus. Her necklace screaming 'FESTIVE' was gleaming like the lights on a Christmas tree.

"Excuse me? Don't tell me you've been snooping on me all the while." I narrowed my eyes.

"I wasn't snooping. Hey, don't look at me like a stalker. I have my life, and I have my way of reading whatever I want to read." She ran her hand through her long mane and gave me a full-body once-over.

"What?"

"Nothing." She shrugged. "I was just thinking about the sacrilege of wasting your time reading steamy romance considering you're still living with Rick Rowling, one of the hottest bachelors in Manhattan. Hey, I have a suggestion. Why not quit reading about a good girl having kinky sex with an alpha male and just do it yourse—"

"Jackie!" I snapped before the ghost of a drag

queen finished her sentence. I would have slapped her, if only she were touchable. Instead, I said, "Hey, I've been thinking about taking exorcism classes from Brian Powers. What do you think?"

"Oh my God, I'm scared," she said flatly.

Then my cell phone chirped. I gave Jackie a menacing glare and took the call. "Hello."

"Hi, Mandy. How are you?" The voice of Daniel Rowling, a.k.a. Dan, trickled into my ear. His voice was deep, smooth, and sexy. Maybe sexier than his son's.

"I'm great. Thank you. So, how have you been?" As I responded, I was almost compelled to add "sir?" but instead I said, "Dan?"

"I'm peachy. Peachier than ever." He chuckled. "By the way, Mandy, I'm glad to be on a first-name basis with you." We weren't video-chatting, but I could see him winking in my mind's eye.

"If you prefer to be addressed as 'sir' or 'Mr. Rowling,' I can switch to them any time." I laughed. Dan was Rick's father and a real-life billionaire CEO of a security-based conglomerate called USCAB—United States Cover All Bases. I used to know him only from his photos in *Forbes* magazine, but when I got to know him in person, he turned out to be quite a friendly guy. "By the way, Rick's at the gym. Do you want me to try calling him?"

"No need to call him. I'm calling you, not my son. Also, I'm good with my current title of Dan. Nothing's as sad as being called 'sir' by my son's girlfriend." He dropped the G-bomb while I was taking a sip of hot tea, catching me by surprise. When I started coughing violently, he asked, "What? Mandy, do you have a cold or something?"

"N-n-no… but, g-g-g-girlfriend?" I stuttered, choking on tea.

"What? Did I say anything wrong?" Dan asked casually. "Considering that you're still living with Rick even after his leg has healed, I'm guessing you and he are an item. Oh, don't tell me you guys haven't yet—"

"So Dan, what's the special occasion for calling me?" I interrupted before he fished for too much information.

My name is Amanda Meyer, but most people, including Dan, call me Mandy. I'm a former medical student turned FBI special assistant. I used to commute to the FBI in Downtown from my parents' home in Queens, but for the past few months, things had drastically changed. I'd sort of moved in to the extravagant condo on Fifth Avenue, the residence of Rick Rowling, my boss.

Unlike what Dan had just said, however, I was only his son's assistant. Under normal circumstances, you didn't cohabitate with your boss, but a twist of fate peppered with a freak accident and a broken ankle brought me to this living arrangement. It was supposed to be temporary until Rick's leg healed, but for some reason, my folks brought some of my stuff to the condo every time they brought dinner and dessert for us. Around the time Rick's leg had actually healed, they decided to tear down my room for renovation so that Emma and Minty, my nieces, could have more sleepovers. And guess what? They knew I was still in debt up to my neck with my student loan and I didn't have money to rent my own space.

Rick had many spare rooms in his 5,000-square-foot condo, and he said I could stay for free if

I occasionally cooked our breakfast. If it were a movie or TV series, we'd be madly in love by now, or at least having kinky sex every day. Still, it was my life and things had never worked out like fiction....

Okay, so there were some moments that had promise to turn out intimate, but every time—and I mean *every* time—something happened to destruct the intimacy. For instance, when we visited Central Park for a picnic, a bomb exploded in the park *and* the ghost of a cold murder case victim pestered me until I told Rick his alleged killer's name. I intended to put the case on hold until Monday, or at least until we finished kissing and what might have followed it, but the ghost was so impatient. Oh, and then there's Jackie constantly popping up from out of nowhere. Anyway, neither of us had uttered the big L-word to each other, and nowadays, I often found myself wondering if perhaps romance didn't mix well with my life.

"Okay, let's talk about the special occasion." As I silently went on and on about the potential issues in my mind, I could picture Dan grinning. "Have you heard of Violet Huss?"

"Of course," I said casually. "Everyone has heard of her. She's famous, you know." I didn't say I was in the middle of devouring her romance novel.

"Excellent. You saved me some explanation. Next Saturday, I've got a dinner date with Violet, and Mandy, you're invited. Be sure to bring Rick with you to make it a double date," he said matter-of-factly, his words sounding more like a statement than a suggestion.

"Ohmygawd! You're having dinner with Violet Huss! I'm sooo jealous!" Jackie shrieked by my ear.

"That'll be brilliant, but I have to ask Rick about his schedule," I said, fighting the urge to shush Jackie and do some tippy-toed happy dance. *Oh my God! I'm invited to a dinner with Violet Huss!*

"Come on, Mandy." Dan *tsked*. "All you need to do is ask him out for dinner. He'll come. Six thirty at Per Se. If the guy says no, you just give me a call. I'll make him come. Your hotline with me is open 24/7. Are we cool?"

"Yes, we're cool," I said. I wasn't sure if Rick was cool about this double date arrangement with his dad, but I wanted to have a dinner with Violet Huss.

"Good. Then I'll see you next week."

We exchanged the usual "have a great weekend" and simultaneously disconnected at the count of three.

* * *

A week later, I was deliriously happy at Per Se.

Eating at one of the most beloved restaurants clad in a little black dress was fun—especially when my date happened to be Rick Rowling. Also, I had become a huge fan of Violet Huss.

Violet was in her early forties, a real woman with the most beautiful violet eyes I'd ever seen. She was sophisticated and a truly awesome person. I asked her a ton of questions—because Jackie urged me to—and Violet always came up with honest but hilarious answers. Indeed, she was hysterically fun, and I found her raspy voice to be totally captivating.

According to Dan, Violet was 'researching' him for her next book featuring a billionaire CEO who was a mortal human.

"Research? What kind of research is that? Talk about smooth words making a difference," Rick muttered into my ear, and I almost snorted mushed and creamed Yukon potato out of my nose. Thank God I didn't end up spewing my dinner all over. I was wearing a good dress for the occasion, and Rick was looking handsome in a black suit and black tie. The suit complimented his 6'2" stature, with long legs supporting a men's underwear model-worthy body. Looking like a toddler after having too much milkshake wasn't high on my to-do list.

Even though Rick's previous comments about his father and his date were cynical, he seemed to be enjoying the evening. I was so grateful that, when our eyes met, I whispered, "Thanks for coming."

"My pleasure." As he whispered back, his mesmerizing green eyes twinkled. At first, he was reluctant about this double-date arrangement, but he agreed to come with me when I told him how much I wanted to see Violet Huss in person.

When the dessert and coffee/tea were served to our table, Dan and Violet exchanged glances.

Rick suddenly looked at his phone. "Oh, crap. Looks like we have a new case. I'd like to stay longer, but we have to leave." He stood up and took my arm.

"But Rick, I didn't notice any incoming messages," I pointed out and reached for my phone. More importantly, I hadn't had dessert, which looked more than tempting. But before I could check for the messages, my eyes widened. "Wha—mmm!" Rick shut me up by kissing me on the lips while helping me to my feet.

"Wait a minute, Richard Alexander Rowling."

Dan *tsked* before our lips parted. "If you're seriously thinking about sneaking out by faking a case and kissing your girlfriend, you're a pathetic optimist. Besides, you're not having any cases tonight. I had a word with Hernandez. Now sit down and enjoy the dessert. By the way, I have a favor to ask you."

Rick clicked his tongue. "More like an assignment than a favor. All right, I saw it coming. What do you want?" He sat down and crossed his arms. "If it's about doing some extracurricular work that involves listening to some model or actress going on and on about their crack-headed conspiracy theory, then I suggest you arrange someone else, such as a shrink."

"Ha. I'm not talking about something so vain. By the way, seeing the two of you getting cozy was a good change in the mood, although you convinced me that I'm a far better kisser than you, young man. If you ask me nicely, I can show you how to kiss a girl properly." Dan winked.

"Hey, old man, don't forget that I'm carrying a gun," Rick said calmly, but the veins were bulging in his neck.

"So what? I have an army of soldiers in the name of USCAB employees." Dan raised an eyebrow.

Fretting uncomfortably on my chair, I glanced at Dan, and then I moved my gaze to Rick. When our eyes met, Rick said under his breath, "See? That's why I prefer dining with your folks rather than with this old thug." I noticed he didn't deny his father's previous comments about yours truly being his girlfriend, which brought a smile to my face. Then he turned to Dan. "You used Violet as bait so Mandy could persuade me to come here. Who's the sneaky one?"

"Sneaky? I'd prefer the term 'strategically calculated.'" Dan shrugged. "Mandy, you should eat the chocolate torte before the ice cream melts away. It's the signature dessert of this place, and having it go to waste is a sacrilege. You can eat Rick's, too. He's busy complaining. Perhaps he's going through another rebellious phase."

"Um… well…." I fidgeted with my words while Jackie commented, "Now I know whose smart-ass gene Rick inherited," which almost prompted me to snort whipped cream out of my nostrils.

"Stop telling her what to do. She's *my* date, not yours," Rick butted in. "Hey, Mandy, stop grinning like an idiot."

Jackie sighed by my side. "In my opinion, Dan's great at driving his son mad every once in a while. Rick looks extra sexy when he's annoyed," she whispered in my ear.

In *my* opinion, Rick was the spitting image of Dan, and I blamed their resemblance for their occasional father-son disagreement.

While I watched the two Rowling men engaging in a verbal duel, Violet was savoring the yummy dessert with one hand and taking notes on her phone with the other like crazy.

"Dan, Rick, thank you so much for this wonderful evening. Guess what? I've just written up a great scene," Violet said in a chipper tone in the middle of the Rowlings' disagreement.

"Isn't that great?" Patting his date's shoulder, Dan winked.

"You're welcome. I'm glad to help," Rick said, as if his previous words and the bulging veins were just for show.

"By the way, have any of you heard about this author, Carina Christien?" Violet asked abruptly.

"I recognize the name, but that's about it," Rick said curtly before taking a big bite of chocolate torte.

"I've read a few of her books. She's a famous author specializing in a horror-mystery hybrid with a touch of paranormal," I added.

Carina Christien was one of those shining stars in the literary industry. Her paranormal occult mysteries were hysterically popular among young adults, ranging from high school students to housewives. If I recalled correctly, some of her books had been turned into motion pictures.

Also, Carina Christien herself was quite a celebrity, being featured in big-name magazines. The photos of her writing new books clad in Goth-princess fashion practically blew my mind. Basically, she was known as a rock star who kicked ass by writing murders.

"She's taken a hiatus from her work, hasn't she?" I asked.

"Right," Violet said. "I heard she decided to take some time off before she burned out. A smart move, I guess."

"I see. Her fans must be dying to read her new books."

"Oh, you mean the Carinists? Yeah, I think they're totally going crazy while waiting for her next book," Violet agreed. "Carina rocks."

"By the way, Carina's former editor is now in charge of Violet," Dan interjected. "He used to manage mystery authors, but he's been recently transferred to the erotica division."

Considering Carina's publisher was one of the

largest, with many departments and divisions, personnel reshuffle seemed to be common.

"Carina is having a public reading, and she wants you, Rick, to attend this event as a guest," Violet said.

"Why me?" Rick frowned.

"You'll see when you get there." Dan smiled mysteriously. "Considering your reputation as the hottest crime fighter in the city, I wouldn't be surprised if she specifically requested your presence."

"Does she want to research me or something?" Rick cocked his head to the side. "In that case, I know a better candidate. Violet, your date tonight used to be called the hottest crime fighter in the city back in the old days. I have a hunch that Carina would be happier having the two of you over to her reading."

"I'd like to volunteer and spare you the trouble, but unfortunately, I already have plans for that day." Dan shook his head.

"I know it's a bold request, but I'm talking about Carina Christien. She has to have you over for the reading *when*, and not if, she wishes so. The publisher simply can't say no to her demands. I heard she's invited her former editor who of course, couldn't say no to her invitation. " Violet shrugged. "Gee, I want to be just like Carina when I grow up."

"Like, the diva who writes steamy romance?" Dan chuckled playfully, prompting Violet to say, "Hmm, that will make a good title, won't it?"

Rick rolled his eyes.

"Hey, you can bring Mandy with you. It'll be fun and romantic," Dan said, turning to us.

"Romantic? What part of a bloody murder mystery makes it romantic, or even fun?" Rick raised an eyebrow and snorted. "In most books and movies, when some bestselling mystery author has a reading party, someone gets killed in the same manner as the murder or murders in the book of the day. Besides, assuming from the author's diva personality, I wouldn't be surprised if she gets whacked."

"The reading will be held at Chateau Hotel and Spa in Tarrytown," Dan went on, totally ignoring Rick's reluctance. Again, I could see where my boss's aggressiveness came from.

"The Chateau Hotel and Spa by the Hudson?" Before Rick responded, I inadvertently perked up. I had heard so many nice things about this mock-European castle built by a newspaper mogul at the turn of the 20th century.

Dan snapped his fingers and produced an envelope from his jacket pocket. "Here's an early Christmas gift for you, Mandy. It's a spa and lunch package scheduled on December 24th. Enjoy!"

"Why, thank you so much!" I accepted the envelope, catching Rick flinching and massaging his temple from the corner of my eye.

Then Dan turned to Rick. "If I were you, I wouldn't send her to Tarrytown on her own. Someone can steal her, especially when she's sporting a post-facial treatment glow. Not to mention this package is for two people, and I've reserved the best shiatsu massage therapist for you. So don't miss this opportunity. You broke an ankle this summer, remember? And guess what? This time of year, filled with chills and snow, is the least kind to old injuries, but a good shiatsu makes a huge difference. Anyway, the reading starts at 6:00 p.m. on the same day. I suggest you guys arrive early. The invitation is in that envelope, Mandy."

"All right, so I'll attend the reading," Rick growled. "Why do I feel trapped?"

"Stop grumbling, young man. Just in case, I've booked a suite so the two of you can relax. Don't worry, it's only an hour drive from the city, and you'll make it to the Christmas party with Mandy's folks." Dan grinned like the Cheshire cat.

CHAPTER 2

Following the double date, I waited for Christmas Eve like a little kid counting how many nights to sleep until opening the Christmas gifts, and the day came much sooner than I'd anticipated.

The Chateau Hotel and Spa didn't disappoint. When I caught a glimpse of the stone building shaped like an old European castle standing atop the peaks in Westchester, I felt as if I had wandered into 18th century Scotland. Or at least a movie set in Hollywood shooting some historical romance flicks. Considering the drive from Manhattan took less than an hour, the experience qualified as magic.

As Dan had told us, the spa turned out to be fantastic. I was scrubbed, massaged, and polished, and by the time my session had ended, I was smelling good. Rick was initially reluctant for the day's plan, but when he finished, he was totally delighted with the result.

After the spa session and late lunch, Rick and I had a stroll in the garden until the cold weather drove us back to the Garden Room in the restaurant. I was dying to look at the room, but unfortunately, ours was reserved with a late check-in plan and visiting the room had to wait. As it was winter, the garden was mostly devoid of greenery and flowers, but reading Carina Christien's books close to the fountains and sculptures, which looked creepy under the cloudy weather, enhanced their eerie tone.

Under normal circumstances, Jackie should

have shrieked joyously at the spa, restaurant, and everything, but on this day, she wasn't tagging along with me. She had a party with other ghosts she'd met in the past few months. She also claimed that she had a date after the party. According to her, it was common for dead people's spirits to come back to the world on Halloween and then stay for the entire holiday season. And during the holiday season, dead people had lots of crazy parties just like we humans did. I didn't know which was weirder—the fact that I regarded having Jackie around me as normal, or that dead people threw parties and dated. Anyway, I was learning new things every day.

"That was impressive," Rick said as he finished the third book by Carina Christien for the day. Seeing him catching up with even the most trivial details about each case by just taking a glance at a case file, I knew his reading speed was superfast, but finishing three books in a day was more impressive to me. "I had this preconception that her books would be childish, but I was wrong. The author's dry sense of humor somehow enhances the creepiness of the stories that always end up catastrophic. Though the whodunit part was easy to tell in every book, the story was well-developed and the culprits' insanity made me smile, especially this story about a restaurant owner who served his previous customers to new customers. It was like Agatha Christie meets Alice Cooper."

"Um." I cleared my throat. "In my universe, such a concept is considered gross." Besides, Carina Christien's books were famous for keeping her readers wondering who the killer was, but I didn't tell that to him. Rick Rowling was notorious for his ruthless approach to investigation, but at the same time, even those who loathed him had to admit his brilliance and be impressed by his case-closure rate, which was slightly higher than 100 percent. I knew that sounded outrageous, but indeed, Rick achieved this whooping number by totally ditching respect toward bureaucracy.

"Oh yeah?" He chuckled. "I'm almost thankful for this occasion."

"I'm glad you changed your opinion. You liked the massage, and I'm sure we'll have a ton of fun at the reading," I said, "with a little touch of dark fantasy, of course."

"You don't understand my old man. When that guy sends me on an errand, you have to expect some snafu." He crossed his long legs in a relaxed manner.

"Still, there's a first time for everything. Let's hope for the best. It's almost Christmas, and perhaps Dan has arranged this little getaway thoroughly as a Christmas gift."

"You have a point." He touched his right ankle where he had a hairline fracture back in the summer. "At least the slight tightness I'd had for a while seems to be gone for now. That alone makes this trip worth our time."

"That's fantastic!" I gently patted his knee.

"I know." He took my hand in his. I half expected Jackie to pop up and butt in between us like she always did, and I instinctively looked around. "What?"

"Oh, it's nothing. I was just thinking like, 'hmm… Jackie must really have a hot date considering she hasn't shown up by now.'"

"Yeah, right. She can be a pain in the ass sometimes." Rick chuckled and glanced at the grandfather clock in the corner of the room. "What time does the door open?"

"Let me see." I took the invitation out of my purse and handed it to him. "The door opens at 5:30 p.m., and the reading starts at 6:00 p.m."

"It's 5:32 p.m., so the door should be open. Let's go."

As we stood up, I caught a glimpse of the garden outside of the windows. The twilight moon lit up the garden with the backdrop of the sky, which was divvied into orange and navy.

It was breathlessly enchanting, but at the same time, I felt somewhat uneasy… like I knew something evil was lurking in the dark corner of the garden.

* * *

The reading was going to be held in another building called the Serene Cottage. According to the hotel's website, the cottage was built about seventy years ago. We walked across the moonlit garden to the large two-story building that looked more like a Gothic mansion rather than a cottage.

The door was open, and people were already coming in.

Just inside the door, the registration desk was set up.

"Hello. Welcome to the Soiree of the Undead." The receptionist manning the registration smiled at us as we entered the cottage. Wearing a black dress with lots of frills and ribbons, she had long, straight, dark hair, and she'd put on heavy makeup with crimson lips contrasting her alabaster complexion. Her eyes matched her lips with the use of crimson contact lenses. It was hard to tell her age, and the woman practically looked like a Goth princess. Somehow, her fashion matched really well with the place, in a horror movie kind of way.

"May I see your ticket or invitation?" she said.

"Sure." Rick presented the invitation.

"Thank you." The receptionist looked at it. "Mr. Rowling, we were looking forward to having you. Please go this way and to the upstairs area. The reading will be held at the café." She indicated her right side at the grand staircase.

We nodded our thanks to her and headed straight to the grand staircase with wood-carved handrails embellished with detailed reliefs.

From the corner of my eye, I caught the person registering after us paying the receptionist.

When we reached the upstairs, my eyes traveled the café floor.

The dark wood floor was shining, reflecting the soft lights. Five wooden tables, made of lighter tones, were set up. Each table had a transparent vase holding a single red rose. The walls were spotless white, which made an eye-catching contrast with the wooden window frame in the same color as the floor. A small Tiffany chandelier cast soft light. In front of the wall with the window was a sofa upholstered in oxblood red.

"This is so beautiful," I murmured. "Imagine Carina Christien herself reciting one of her stories—not the spooky one, but a romantic one."

"Seriously? Personally, I'd prefer to listen to something featuring a deranged, murderous clown." Rick chuckled as he pulled a chair out for me at a table.

"Thanks. I'm not a huge fan of clowns, but

they are such a rave among her readers."

"Clowns are seriously disturbing, and they're huge megahit factors in horror stories."

"I know." I nodded. "Speaking of megahit, did you know that Carina Christien started her writing career in a rather humble way? One of New York's publishers hosted a contest to discover new authors, and she won second place when she was a theater arts school student. The prize for her achievement was just a thousand bucks."

"Seriously? That's unbelievable." He raised an eyebrow.

"I know. Back then, she wasn't regarded as a future star, but her story got glowing reviews when featured in a magazine, so they had her add some more scenes and elements and republished as a book, which hit the *New York Times* and *USA Today* bestseller lists. Her book sold explosively, and the rest is history."

"Talk about a Cinderella story."

While we chatted at the table, a tall guy in his early thirties approached us. "You must be Rick Rowling," he said eagerly.

"Yes?" Rick glanced at him. "Have we met before?"

"Oops, where are my manners? I'm Dylan Woodhouse, an editor at Roseberry House. I'm currently in charge of Violet Huss. Nice to meet you." With a smile, Woodhouse offered his hand to Rick. As he did, Woodhouse emphasized his height by bending his knees.

"Nice meeting you, too." Rick stood up to shake hands with Woodhouse. "I heard so much about you from Violet," he said, demonstrating that he was even taller than the editor.

"I'm so glad you could make it here. I really appreciate it." Woodhouse's smile widened. "You know what? You practically saved my behind. Carina caught a rumor about you, and she insisted on having you for this occasion. When she wants something, she has to have it no matter what. I owe a lot to Violet, I guess. Without her I would have had no luck having you here. Now I can understand her insistence. Her adoration for sexy men like you borders on obsession." As he spoke, he looked more like someone from the TV industry rather than a literary editor.

"Should I be flattered or what?" Rick tilted his head to the side.

Woodhouse moved his gaze toward me. "Look at your cute date."

"This is Miss Amanda Meyer," Rick introduced me. When he continued, "She lives with me," my jaw dropped. I looked at him in surprise. He responded with a lopsided smile and sat down.

"Oh, what a shame. She's taken." Woodhouse chuckled. "Good thing you told me that before I asked her out. Hello, Amanda." As he extended his hand toward me, I felt nervous. In my previous life as a medical student, three of my patients dropped dead just minutes after touching me, and since then, I wasn't comfortable shaking hands with a total stranger. The series of unfortunate incidents had me kicked out of med school, and monikered with an even more unfortunate nickname, the Grim Reaper. Thanks to my nickname, no one except for Rick Rowling at the FBI ever offered their hands for a handshake.

"I see a ring on your ring finger, but I don't see your date. Where is she?" Rick interjected as I froze without taking Woodhouse's hand.

"Um, yes. My wife's staying home. After all, we have a four-month-old child and this event didn't seem to be baby-friendly. We had a shotgun marriage, but I wasn't really expecting such a sudden marriage or becoming a father." He touched the ring with his previously extended right hand and shrugged nonchalantly.

Having passed the awkwardness of shaking hands, I felt sorry for his wife as I caught reluctance crossing his face. At the same time, I was slightly tempted to kick him in the behind. It took two people to have a baby, and he was acting like it wasn't his choice. Talk about an immature guy!

As I fretted with my thoughts about a total stranger's marriage, waitstaff at the café started beverage and snack service with a wagon full of assorted teas, coffee, scones and clotted cream, sandwiches, and heavenly selections of petit fours.

I looked around and saw only eight people, including us. There were a couple of women in their midtwenties, two men accompanying the women, and another older guy in a leather jacket and motorcycle pants. As for the older guy, he looked the least happy for the occasion.

"It looks like a small group reading. Is this some kind of an experimental session?" Rick asked Woodhouse.

"Actually, Carina's been totally secretive about this reading, so I don't know much about it other than she wanted you to be here."

"Did she tell you why?" Rick asked, swiping his phone.

"Unfortunately, no." Woodhouse shook his head. I caught a slight irritation in his voice. "She's kind of kept me out of the loop."

"Speaking of uncommunicative, there's no announcement about this reading on her official website." Rick showed the screen to us. Carina's website was dramatically eye-catching. The background was bloodred, and an animated white rose shed its white petals.

"What would you like to drink?" I caught one of the staff asking the women at the next table.

"Can I have champagne?"

"I'm sorry, ma'am, but alcoholic beverages can be served only after the reading. The sponsor of this event wants to make sure that everyone can concentrate," the female waitstaff—a college student, perhaps—said apologetically.

"Okay, then I'll have a coffee."

When the waitstaff came to our table, Rick ordered Earl Grey, and I had a Hibiscus tea and a red velvet truffle.

Woodhouse, who took a seat at our table, took a sip of coffee and talked to me. "Hmm, red beverage and red chocolate. Amanda, you must be a true red aficionado."

"I should have ordered a mint julep truffle instead," I said. "The green would have added more holiday flair."

As I responded, a couple of women at the next table waved at Woodhouse.

"Hi, Dylan."

"Why don't you introduce us to your friends?"

Woodhouse waved back at them. "This is Amanda and Rick Rowling." Then he introduced the women to us. "This is Catherine Davenport, and the lady here is Natalia Rain. They're Carina's BFFs from high school and my occasional heroes in times of need."

"Rick Rowling? The USCAB heir? Oh my God! Haven't I seen him on Page Six? Dylan, you've got to tell us how you're acquainted with him," Catherine said excitedly as Natalia quietly displayed a neutral smile by her side. Obviously, Catherine was outgoing and Natalia seemed reserved.

"Violet Huss, my currently hottest author, is a friend of his father," Woodhouse responded.

"Oh, yes. Violet can be pretty persuasive." Rick displayed a polite smile like he was genuinely happy and enjoying this conversation.

"It's so lovely meeting you!" Catherine extended her hand.

When Rick said, "Pleased to meet you," and shook her hand, I caught a glimpse of his façade as the successor of his family's multibillion conglomerate.

After shaking hands with him, Catherine happily called to one of the guys chatting by the wall. "Hey, Harry. You should come meet Rick."

As the young guy—perhaps in his early twenties—scurried to her side, Catherine introduced him. "This is Harry Geiser, a photographer. I think it'd be nice if Harry could shoot your photos for *Forbes* magazine." Then she turned to Harry. "Meet Rick Rowling. He's the USCAB heir."

"My photos for *Forbes* magazine?" Rick shook his head. "No one at *Forbes* wants my photos, I'm afraid. They don't have time to feature a civil servant in their magazine." I didn't miss a slight twitch of his eyebrows as he said that.

"I'm sorry, Rick," Harry apologized. "Catherine has this tendency of overpromoting me to everyone she sees. Besides, my boss over there is the main photographer. I'm just his assistant. My work with Carina is more of a web designer rather than a photographer."

"Come on, Harry. Grab your chance while she's still pushing you for your success." The guy who had been chatting with Harry by the wall ambled toward Harry and chimed in. "Perhaps she's trying to boost your confidence by upgrading your portfolio. My gut instinct says Catherine's waiting for you to pop the question."

"Tyson, I respect you as my boss, but please let me make my life's decisions, okay?" Harry looked troubled following his boss's words, but I saw a hint of a smile crossing Catherine's face.

"Hmm… in that case, you can shoot photos of my old man," Rick said, smiling like a cat licking cream. "Perhaps dressing him up in an Easter bunny suit or something will capture the world's attention."

"Are you sure USCAB's CEO would dress up in an Easter bunny suit and let me take photos of him?" Harry asked with a serious face.

"I don't know, but personally, I'd love to see it," Rick responded.

"Rick," I whispered into his ear, "I don't think Dan would like to appear on magazines in a bunny suit."

"I know, but there's a first time for everything." He flashed a wicked grin.

Shaking my head, I took a glance at the man in motorcycle wear. While Carina's acquaintances—Dylan Woodhouse, Catherine, Natalia, Harry, and his boss called Tyson—chatted away, he was impatiently tapping his feet while seated.

"Come on, give me a break! How long is she going to make me wait?" He angrily kicked one of the table's legs.

"Excuse me, you are…?" Woodhouse asked him in a puzzled manner.

"I'm Larry Burton, a P.I. I did two gigs for Carina Christien. My reports were flawless, but she refused to pay for one of the assignments, telling me she wasn't satisfied with the results. She'd been ghosted away, and then, all of a sudden, I'm summoned to this reading. I don't know what the hell is going on," he answered, irritably scratching his head.

"Wh-what was that assignment about?" Woodhouse asked. For some reason, his voice went an octave higher, as if channeling Mickey Mouse.

"Have you ever heard of confidentiality?" Glaring at the people gathering around, the P.I. flashed a grin. The bared incisors gleamed like knives.

CHAPTER 3

As awkwardness filled the air, the lights were dimmed and the sound of high heels clicking on the hardwood floor echoed.

In the eclipsed light, the woman from the registration desk came into the café. She was carrying a candle in one hand.

Everyone stopped chattering, and then came a silence.

"Thank you all for gathering for this special occasion. I'm Kimmie Balman, younger sister of Carina Christien. Tonight, I'm reciting my sister's work." She looked around the tables and walked to the sofa. "Now, let's open the door for the Soiree of the Undead." She bowed and took a seat. As she did, I noticed she was sporting a choker necklace that she didn't have on at the registration desk. The necklace came with a crimson stone—garnet, perhaps—the size of a mushroom.

"Rita's sister? It's my first time seeing her. Have you seen her, Nat?" Catherine whispered to Natalia, who shook her head, muttering, "No. I've never seen her."

I caught them talking and figured that Carina Christien's real name was Rita.

"Rita? Aha, now I understand," Rick murmured and took a sip of tea.

"What do you understand?" I asked him, to which he responded with an enigmatic smile.

Without answering my question, he winked

and touched my lips with his index finger. "We've got to be quiet for the reading."

Feeling my cheeks burning and appreciating the shades, I glanced at Kimmie, who was holding a big, leather-bound book that looked like an ancient manuscript. I found it a romantic theater tool.

As Kimmie blew out the candle, the spotlight above her head switched on. She put the unlit candle on the floor, sat up, and opened her mouth. "I was killed on that day—to be exact, I was murdered."

I knew Kimmie was only reciting the manuscript, but there was something awe-inspiring with the way she uttered those words.

She went on about the tale of a girl who aspired and thrived to become a great actress. The former mousy girl grabbed the chance and turned into an overnight success. She acquired everything— fame, fortune, and a loving boyfriend. However, her happily ever after suddenly ended when she was murdered by someone who envied her success.

"I should remember who killed me. I should have felt the touch of my killer, but unfortunately, I don't seem to recall anything. Perhaps due to the shock I had—as they say, death has a tremendous impact on one's soul." She took a deep breath. "On that night, I was sporting a red velvet ribbon around my neck as I climbed the railing of my condo's balcony and hanged myself. I was still wearing my red shoes, and a neatly typed suicide note with my signature was left on my desk. I had allegedly committed suicide, but actually, I didn't even think about killing myself—which led me to believe that I was murdered. I was definitely murdered by someone listening to my tale." Then Kimmie raised her face and glared at the people sitting in front of her.

At first, it seemed like a typical Carina Christien bit for the show, but when the lights were suddenly turned on, I noticed everyone, except for Rick and I, was sporting a blanched face.

"That was untasteful, wasn't it, Kimmie?" Woodhouse stood up and snapped.

"Yes, that was gross!" Catherine declared. "It's supposed to be a party to celebrate Rita's recovery."

"Or else… are you implying that her condition has changed?" Natalia eyeballed Kimmie suspiciously.

I was having a hard time grasping the situation, but when I caught a glimpse of Larry Burton, the P.I., his mouth was agape as if he were genuinely shocked.

Arms crossed, Kimmie stood up. Glaring around the place, she said, "Okay, so let me tell you a little bit about this gathering for those of you who may be confused. Rita Balman, my sister, achieved huge success as an author named Carina Christien. But all of a sudden, she attempted suicide by hanging herself from the balcony of her office—sporting her usual getup of a black dress, red ribbon choker necklace, and red patent leather shoes. A printed suicide note with her signature was left on the desk in the room.

"Except, she didn't end up dying from suffocation. The noose around her neck loosened and she fell from the balcony, straight to the hard limestone patio floor. Thanks to hitting the large Christmas tree, she didn't die immediately. She was alive when she was found lying unconscious. She was in critical condition and stayed unconscious for three days, but her body and soul chose to live. When she woke up, she strongly denied trying to commit suicide. She declared that someone tried to murder her."

My jaw dropped. This was supposed to be a romantic getaway, and another murder attempt was the last thing I'd expected—no, I mean, dreaded! I glanced at Rick, who was casually listening to Kimmie's story.

"Catherine, Natalia, you two were at Rita's office that night just before the incident. Dylan, you were having a personal issue with my sister, weren't you?" Kimmie pointed her accusing finger at each person. "Tyson, you had a phone conversation just seconds before her fall, and Harry, you should have been there when she fell from the balcony. And, oh, Mr. Burton, Rita told me how you shouted at her and threatened to kill her."

"What the hell are you talking about? That woman hired me, I did my assignments with detailed reports, and then she changed her mind, saying she wouldn't pay for my work. Can you just say, 'Okay. I understand. Have a great day!' Who am I? Polly-fucking-anna?" Burton, the P.I., banged the table. "Besides, they were just words. Talking about killing and actually killing are two different things!"

"I'm an editor! Sometimes the editing process can be a hell of a rough ride, and there are times I have no choice but to make some harsh comments. Still, if she jumped off the balcony following an argument with me, that doesn't make me a killer, does it?" Woodhouse yelled.

"He's right!" Catherine chimed in. "Okay, so sometimes, Natalia and I were a little envious of Rita, but that doesn't make us killers. On that day, Rita was totally stressed out, and we got worried. So we went to her favorite gourmet food place to buy some cakes, only to find her lying unconscious. Oh, did you just forget that we're the ones who called the ambulance?"

"Yeah, right. What good does it make for us to kill Rita?" Natalia crossed her arms angrily.

Tyson Owen, the photographer, shook his head and let out an exasperated snort. On the other hand, his assistant, Harry Geiser, was at a loss for words and was visibly shaking.

"You know what? I just called Carina Christien for a work-related thing, and Kimmie, you're accusing me of attempted murder?" Tyson said.

"It's not just a murder *attempt*. I'm talking about a murder," Kimmie shot back. "Rita had been recovering, but she sustained brain aneurysms due to the head injury she suffered from the fall. Her condition had been up and down and then three days ago, she started to deteriorate, and now… she's gone! 'Find my killer' were her final words before she slipped back into a coma, and then she died. So here I came, sticking with her initial plan to identify the person who pushed her before the media finds out about her death!"

Tyson turned pale, but he managed to say, "I'm sorry for your loss. Still, if you're accusing us of her death, can you at least demonstrate who did that to her and how?"

Kimmie displayed a calm, sad smile. "I'm not capable of identifying my sister's killer, so I called Rick Rowling, the top-notch FBI agent who's also known as New York City's answer to Sherlock Holmes. He can see through one's mind and solves every case as soon as he sets his foot at the crime scene. Mr. Rowling, please solve my sister's murder. I will offer the best possible compensation to you."

Rick turned to me and whispered, "Did you just hear her words? You must be impressed."

"Hey, I think I'm helping you a lot with your cases," I whispered back.

Everyone's eyes were on Rick, as if he were under the spotlight. Just as the stress level reached a whole new high, he flashed a wicked grin. "Fine. If you insist, let me try my best for this case."

I was taken aback by his eagerness. I'd never known Rick Rowling as someone with a voluntary spirit. Given his reluctance when Dan tried to persuade him into attending this occasion, I couldn't help feeling nervous.

"Rick." I touched his arm. "You're not thinking about deliberately messing up this case just to punish Dan, are you?"

For a split second, he fell silent. "I have no intention of punishing anyone. Let's just call it a 'make a point' project. Suppose things don't work out as my old man planned. Then he wouldn't think of sending me as a handyman," he whispered back.

"I don't think that's a good idea. We're talking about a murder, after all. Besides, if your reputation is crushed, then USCAB's will be crushed, too."

"You're exaggerating."

"Excuse me? What are you talking about?" Catherine said impatiently.

"Fine. I'll try solving this case." Then he turned to Kimmie. "Okay, let's get it done quickly."

"Thank you." Kimmie's face slightly perked up.

Rick stood up and ambled toward Kimmie.

The sound of his leather-soled loafers clicking the wood floor echoed.

As he stood by Kimmie's side, he turned to the crowd. "Here's the thing. Unlike how Kimmie has previously described me, I'm just an ordinary human. And her story about me finger-pointing the culprit the moment I set foot in the crime scene was cool, except it was a total overstatement. As for the case, I need to understand more about the background, so I'll ask each of you a few questions one by one, and then I'll tell you my opinion. Are we cool with that?"

People exchanged glances and nodded in agreement.

CHAPTER 4

"Thank you," Rick said like a gentleman. I had a hunch that the people attending this reading had no idea that he had once grabbed a suspect by his hair and shook him, and by the time he fessed up, the suspect was 70 percent bald. "Before questioning each of you, Kimmie, can you walk me through the context?"

Kimmie visibly strained. Gulping the air and clenching her fists, she started. "Exactly a year ago, on the night of Christmas Eve, my sister hanged herself at the condo she had been using as an office. She wrapped a long, bloodred ribbon around her neck and then jumped off the balcony on the fifth floor. But the ribbon loosened and she fell, straight to the concrete below. Still, the huge Christmas tree caught her, saving her for the time being. She had a bad concussion and didn't remember what happened at the time of the incident."

When Kimmie finished talking, Rick abruptly said, "By the way, I heard that Carina Christien was originally from the West Coast, but now she lives in New York. Did she move to the city following her literary success?"

"No. After graduating from high school in the suburb of Seattle, she went to junior college, specializing in theater arts, in New York City."

"Okay, so she used to be in Washington until college. And what about you, Kimmie? Where do you live currently?"

"I live in my sister's place in Midtown. Rita invited me to live with her a while after her debut as an author. I'm like her homemaker, assisting her with cooking, laundry, accounting, and so on."

"I see. That's why your sister has an office— to have her alone time."

"Exactly." Kimmie nodded with a slightly relaxed manner.

"When did you learn about the incident with your sister?"

"Dylan, my sister's editor back then, gave me a call when Rita was being rushed to the hospital. After that, things got rough with hospital registration, talking to the police, and everything." Kimmie furrowed her eyebrows, as if she were regurgitating the bitter taste of the memory.

I could imagine her anxiety and stomach-churning feelings. I used to be a medical student before I started working with Rick. I used to believe I'd seen too much sorrow and despair at hospitals to be scared of visiting them. But I was wrong. When I accompanied Rick to the hospital in the summer when he got hurt, I felt so worried that I cried.

"How did you learn your sister had her friends, Catherine and Natalia, visiting her at the time of the incident?"

"From the detectives I talked to," Kimmie replied. "Also, Tyson made two phone calls prior to Rita's fall."

"Not just once, but twice." Rick crossed his arms in thought.

"Hey, don't get me wrong," Tyson, the photographer, chimed in. "I made the second call because there was something I missed on my first call. That's all."

"About that. You can save it for later until we'll have a private talk," Rick told the photographer, and he turned to Kimmie again. "So, Kimmie, what brought you to hold a reading in this way instead of alerting the police to an attempted murder immediately after her fall?"

Following a brief silence, she said, "When Rita woke up, she made me promise never to publicize her mishap. After that, she clammed up, so I was almost convinced that she had actually tried to commit suicide. But one day, she said, 'I was almost murdered, and I need your help finding my killer,' and she told me about this project she'd been developing. She said the whole purpose of this gathering was revealing the assailant."

"So, she invited them here, setting the celebration of her recovery as the surface reason. And, even her death didn't stop you from executing her plan." Rick uncrossed his arms. His face was unreadable.

"No, it didn't."

"And you also noted that Rita, a.k.a. Carina, had no memory about the night of her fall, right?"

"Exactly." Kimmie nodded.

"I see."

As Rick looked at the attendees, I observed them carefully. No one started to make a tearful confession, but the jitters were palpable. If Kimmie's accusation was right and the assailant was there, the person must have been relieved with the information about Carina's memory loss. Or maybe the purpose of the assailant attending might have been to check if Carina's memory had been really lost.

Anyway, the series of events couldn't get weirder. Speaking of weirdness, I couldn't help noticing something—or rather, noticing something missing. I had to talk to Rick about that, but before I had a chance, he said, "All right, now let me run individual interviews. Catherine, can I start with you?"

"Of course." She displayed a flirty smile that made me wonder what drove Carina Christien to befriend her in the first place.

"Okay, so Catherine, Kimmie, and Mandy will be staying here, and the rest of you can go downstairs and wait for your turns," Rick said matter-of-factly, and the others left the café without arguing. Considering the previous bitter reaction from multiple attendees, it felt almost magical that they followed his orders.

"Rick, can I have a word with you?" Before he started interrogating Catherine, I pulled him to the corner of the café where she and Kimmie couldn't hear us.

"What?" He raised an eyebrow.

"We need Jackie's help," I whispered to him.

"Help from Jackie? No. I don't think so." He shook his head.

"But this case is weird. Kimmie said her sister's dead, but I can't feel death from her. Perhaps Jackie will be better for this case. She's dead, so she might be better at talking to newly dead people than me."

"You don't understand. Carina's not dead," he said nonchalantly.

"Excuse me?" My eyes widened.

"I saw Carina's photos and felt no death either." He swiped his phone and showed me an image of Carina in a bathtub filled with crimson liquid that reminded the viewer of blood. "She's fine.

She won't be dying anytime soon."

"But—"

"Oh, come on. Stop Jackie-ing. I can tell if a person is dead or alive when I see the photo, remember?" he said, silencing me by touching my lips with his fingers.

I nodded.

"Remember what?" Jackie asked, popping up from out of nowhere, carrying a paper bag in one hand and holding a fried chicken drumstick in another.

"Oh, we're talking about Rick's special skill to see a person's vital status by looking at the photograph," I replied and then jumped a foot. "Jackie! What are you doing here?"

"Hello? That's not the reaction I expect from someone who repeatedly called my name." She wiggled her greasy fingers.

"Is Jackie here?" Rick asked, and when I nodded, he groaned. "How's she doing?"

"She looks perky as always." Then I turned to the ghost of a drag queen sporting a red and white Christmas hat. "How are you doing?"

"I'm good. Oh, did I mention I was having a blast at the party until a minute ago?" Jackie said, between chewing the chicken. "I met this ghost of a Japanese lady, Mariko, who's hosting a really fab party! Did you know Japanese people eat tons of fried chicken and really yummy and lovely cakes on Christmas Eve? According to Mariko, kids open their presents on Christmas morning, but the rest of the day goes normal with people going to work or school."

"Wow, that's impressive," I said and relayed Jackie's words to Rick.

"I didn't know dead people eat chickens and

cakes," he said.

"It's special perks during the holiday seasons. Between Halloween and New Year's Day, we get to eat and drink, but unlike when you're alive, you don't get too drunk. Want to try some?" Jackie offered her bag of chicken to us.

"Thanks for offering, but no," I declined, mostly because I was afraid that I might join Deadville if I sampled their food. Still, it was a tempting offer since the chicken smelled oh-so-heavenly. "Hey, I like your FESTIVE necklace. It's extra lovely in red, white, and green."

"I know!" She beamed. "So, can I go?"

"Oh, of course, you can go and enjoy the party—" I said, but Rick interrupted me.

"Wait a minute," he said. "Several people are gathering downstairs. Can you go and snoop on their conversation before you go back to the party?"

"Of course. I've got to burn some calories." Jackie winked and floated out of the café toward the stairs. I didn't know dead people had to worry about calories.

"All right. Now let's start interrogating." He rolled his shoulders.

"Questioning," I rephrased, touching his arm.

"Whatever." He shrugged. "Hey, when Jackie reports something to you, just text me, okay? And no gasping."

"Fine," I said, looking up at his mesmerizing green eyes. "Should I take a sign language course?"

"Very funny." He snorted, but his eyes were shimmering with laughter.

When we went back to the interview, Kimmie and Catherine were sitting at different tables, looking uncomfortable. As we approached them, Kimmie let out a sigh and Catherine batted her eyelashes at Rick. "Oh, you're finally back," she said, giving me a flicker of a nasty glare.

Rick went to Catherine's table. "Sorry for keeping you waiting," he said and turned to me. "Mandy, you can sit wherever you like."

I nodded and sat at an empty table where I could see both Kimmie and Catherine.

Catherine seemed slightly tense, but as Rick sat in front of her, she displayed an amused smile. "Oh my God, it's the first time for me to talk to an FBI agent!"

"Oh no. You can forget about the FBI. I'm only here as a fan of Carina Christien." Rick displayed a gentle smile that was reserved for strangers. "So, I heard you're a friend of Carina— let's call her Rita for now—since high school. Can you tell me how you befriended her?"

"Let's see." Catherine looked up at the ceiling and then back at Rick. "Back in high school, I was in the slutty group, sporting heavy makeup and everything. Natalia was a prep girl with excellent grades, aiming for an Ivy League college, and Rita was a shy girl. Under normal circumstances, we wouldn't have noticed each other's presence, but we ended up spending the summer of our freshman year volunteering at a local library. Despite our differences, all of us liked reading. Anyway, we became fast friends." As she talked, her expression softened, like she was indulging herself with a moment of nostalgia.

"Did you guys keep in touch after graduating from high school?" Rick interjected.

"No, we went our separate ways after graduation, and we didn't keep in touch for a while. I went to one of those partying schools, Natalia went to the state university—which wasn't exactly an Ivy League school, but it was great anyway—and Rita moved to New York."

"By the way, Catherine, are you still based on the West Coast?"

"No. Currently, I'm in Union City." She shook her head. "After college, I got a job in Manhattan so I moved to Chelsea, but I relocated across the bridge for more space for less rent. Natalia lives in an apartment just across the street from mine, you know. In her case, she got a job at a local branch office of an insurance company back in Seattle, but she didn't like her company culture, so she quit and moved to the East Coast. She's now working for a consumer products company. I, on the other hand, am at the planning section of a travel agency."

I observed Catherine chattering about things Rick hadn't even asked and decided that she was a born blabbermouth.

"I see. So, when did you reconnect with Rita?"

"Well, it was when Natalia and I were in our sophomore year at college. Rita called me when she was visiting Seattle, saying she wanted to have a reunion. So we lunched, and Rita told us she was writing a story and intended to submit it to publishers. And we were like, 'Good luck!' Her story actually scored an award, so we had a celebration party. And since then, we've been very close."

"So, how did you feel about Rita winning an award?"

"Well, I was like, 'Congrats!' and I guess Natalia felt the same way. It was great that Rita's story was selected, but it only scored second place and the prize was just a thousand bucks. She offered to treat us, using her prize money, but we went Dutch, persuading her to save her hard-earned money." She chuckled, recalling the moment. She sounded like she was simply happy for her friend's achievement.

"Uh-huh." Rick nodded. "By the way, you and Harry are dating, right? How did you two get to know each other?"

"Oh, Harry. You know, as a travel planner who discovers and develops new travel itineraries, I often need photographs in my line of work. So I asked Rita if she knew any good photographers, and she introduced me to Tyson and Harry. As you can see, Tyson's a little sarcastic, though he takes really kick-ass photos. And as for Harry, he's so talented, you know. He's a super-duper designer who makes killer webpages like Rita's official website. Her website changes the theme monthly, and Harry's in charge of everything. Also, he's full of fab ideas, and he's my go-to guy whenever I'm in need of unique ideas. Oh, don't forget that he's the sweetest guy I've ever met. Harry makes me feel safe and secure."

As I listened to her going on about her boyfriend, I was almost compelled to butt in and ask her about how she became so intimate with him. Not that I was that curious about her love life, but I was thinking about *my* love life—or lack thereof. Okay, so I was living with Rick, who made me feel safe and secure—indeed, he protected me from harm's way, not just once but twice—but somehow, something kept us from getting *really* intimate.

Take that Saturday night at a fundraising auction, which Rick attended as a favor for his father who was in Kyoto for business and couldn't make it to the event. That night seemed promising. I was arm in arm with Rick, smiling and mingling with the crowd. The lighting was soft, the ambience was so intimate, and I was seriously anticipating that our relationship would proceed to the next level—that was until one of the auctioned items went missing and the event turned into a jewelry heist case. Of course, Rick solved it in no time, raising several million bucks and acquiring huge leverage. The thief happened to be the wife of a very powerful man in New York, and after obtaining her confession, Rick had a word with her billionaire husband who was more than happy to purchase the item for a ridiculously high price—eight million dollars, to be exact—and promised to accompany his wife to a therapist specializing in kleptomania. While Rick focused on the case, I was ogling a really cute ring. The moment I caught a glimpse of four pieces of pink sapphire shaped into a four-leaf clover over the delicate Art Deco-style gold band, I fell in love with it. The minimum bidding price made me flinch, but I sucked it up and made a bid. At that time, I had been working for the FBI for almost a year, keeping me up-to-date with my student loan payment, so I decided to treat myself.

Anyway, by the time the auction was over, the romantic anticipation had been dead. And oh, did I mention that the pink sapphire ring was sold to some mysterious bidder? The price was far higher than I could afford. I was thankful Rick was elsewhere during the bidding process, because I got a little teary when I lost and I didn't want to get caught reacting like a little kid.

I sighed. I really liked that ring, but having wasted that seemingly promising evening on another investigation did more damage to my ego. The problem was that wherever we went, Rick and I tended to stumble upon a case….

"What's wrong with us? No, it's not us. It's not even me. It's all about the timing. The hexed timing…," I mumbled and groaned while recalling the auction night and other times that ended in unidealistic ways, totally forgetting about the murder.

Rick cleared his throat. "Hexed timing? Mandy, what are you talking about?"

"Um… well…." Yanked back to reality, I fretted with words. "I guess I was a little zoned out. My apologies," I said, prompting Catherine to grin and Rick to raise an eyebrow.

He turned back to Catherine. "Okay, so how did you get acquainted with Dylan Woodhouse?"

At the mention of Rita's former editor, Catherine's grin widened. "The first time I met him was when I was visiting Rita's office. I often crashed her office because I was dying to see him. You know, Rita was totally passionate for him." She winked.

My ears perked. Rita's adoration for the editor was news to me, but Rick just nodded. "Oh, really? I had a hunch about that."

"Seriously? You knew that?" Catherine slightly pouted, tilting her head to the side. "That was the part where you were supposed to be surprised."

"No surprise, unfortunately." Rick shook his head. "Kimmie mentioned that Rita had a personal issue with Dylan, and I assumed the seed of the trouble to be his marriage. Perhaps that's part of the reason why Dylan stepped down as Rita's editor."

"That's right. What a shame. I feel sorry for him. It was just a one-way love for Rita. Considering they weren't even dating, it was a tad bit unfair for her to snap like that the moment she caught the news of Dylan's marriage. I knew she was lacking experience in the dating department, though I didn't think she was that naïve." Catherine went on rambling, despite Kimmie eyeing daggers at her.

"So, on the night of Rita's fall, what were you doing at her office?" Rick asked.

"Like I said, Rita was having a perfect storm over Dylan. She was so out of control, and Natalia and I went to cheer her up. Even then, Rita was acting somewhat weirdly, and we figured some comfort food would help. So we went to Dean & DeLuca to buy some sweets. When we returned to the building, we found Rita on the patio floor… bleeding and… totally motionless." Catherine shut her eyes tightly and frowned as if she were trying to let the painful memory go. "Natalia called the ambulance, and I called Dylan."

"What was the reason for not calling Kimmie at that time?" Rick interjected.

"Because neither of us knew her number. I knew Rita lived with her younger sister, but we didn't know her personally."

"Uh-huh, right. Okay, that's about it for now, Catherine. Thanks for your cooperation. You can go downstairs. Can you please ask Natalia to come up to have a little chat, please?"

"Sure." Catherine smiled. "At first, I was nervous about being interrogated, but it was such a pleasure talking to a good-looking guy like you." She stood up and, on her exit, blew a kiss at Rick, who responded with a polite smile but didn't catch it in midair.

CHAPTER 5

When Catherine left the café, Rick took out his phone and opened Carina Christien's official website.

"Look at those photos featuring a brick house." Rick showed the screen to Kimmie. "I have a hunch that they're tweaked versions of the condo building's exterior of her office, am I correct?"

"Yes. Rita's office is on the fifth floor of an eight-story building. Though it's a brand new project, the exterior is finished with red bricks. The photos have been processed so that you can't pinpoint the exact location of the building."

"I see. Good work by Harry and Tyson, I guess." As Rick nodded, footsteps echoed from the stairs. We stopped talking and watched Natalia entering the café.

"Can you make it quick and simple?" Natalia, who didn't bother with pleasantries or greetings, snapped at Rick. "I don't want to waste my time for this shenanigan."

"Of course, I was thinking the same thing," Rick said, then indicated to the leather upholstered sofa. "Please have a seat."

"Oookay." Slightly grimacing, Natalia sat on the sofa.

"I heard you were the whiz kid back in high school."

"Catherine said that?" Natalia raised her face and furrowed her eyebrows. "Oh, no. We were in a mediocre school, and I was doing slightly better than average. Still, I had a hard time keeping up with other kids at college."

"So it seems like you, Catherine, and Rita were completely different types. What turned the three of you into best friends?" Rick asked the same question he'd asked Catherine. Trying to trip them up, perhaps?

"What brought us close? I'd say volunteering at a local library. All of us loved mysteries, and we spent most of our supposedly working hours discussing books and critiquing authors as if we were the experts." Natalia smiled, looking like she was about to let out a giggle.

"And you guys decided to each try your hand at writing original stories, right?" Rick said matter-of-factly, but I had a hard time keeping my straight face as it was news to me. Catherine never mentioned writing stories. When I glanced at Kimmie, she also seemed to be trying her best not to gasp.

Natalia's shoulders visibly twitched. "Oh, she said that, too? What a blabbermouth." She let out a small sigh. "Actually, Rita was the one who was writing a story. We often saw her scribbling something on a legal pad at slow times, and one day we twisted her arm into showing her notes, guessing it was some kind of love poem addressed to her secret crush. Rita was reluctant, but she finally let us read her work, which turned out to be a novel. It was no masterpiece, totally lacking catharsis and climax, and I remember us teasing her for that, feeling like God Almighty critics."

"And you two joined her in writing, right?" Rick asked.

"Well, I'd rather call it trying my hand at

writing." Natalia shrugged. "So, seeing Rita's work, Catherine said we had to write, too. We started writing but failed miserably. Catherine was good with building characters, but her plotting and sentence structure were below substandard—catastrophic, really. I liked plotting and thinking about the ploy, but my story and characters were so flat and sleepy to the point that I got sick of my own story. So, Catherine and I ended up abandoning the project, and Rita was the only person who wrote it until the end. I still remember how much I respected her for finishing her work instead of permanently leaving it as a work in progress." Natalia looked past us, as if she were savoring the memory.

"By the way, Natalia, you're currently based in New Jersey, right? What brought you there from Seattle?" As Rick changed the subject, Natalia fell silent. After a pause, he added. "Did your friends' presence on the East Coast play a part in your relocation?"

A cynical smile crossed Natalia's lips. "Well, I had some unpleasant memories back home, and I was compelled to get out of my home state where I grew up, just like Rita. Then again, I was wary of going someplace where I knew no one, so I decided to move close to Rita and Catherine."

"Just like Rita? What do you mean?"

"Oh, Catherine didn't tell that? Rita's parents got a divorce when she was a freshman in high school, and both of them remarried as soon as the divorce was settled. So her home wasn't really a home, and she was often picked on in school. She wanted a fresh start at a place no one knew her. That's why she went to New York."

"I see," Rick muttered and looked at Kimmie,

as if to check Natalia's story.

"She's right," Kimmie said. "Things like our parents' divorce drove Rita out of our hometown. As soon as her writing took off, she took me under her wing by inviting me to live with her in Manhattan. Rita has never told our parents about her success, so they still don't know what she has accomplished as Carina Christien."

"Still? She was proactively revealing herself to the media, wasn't she?" Rick questioned, puzzled.

"Rita's Goth fashion has two purposes: one is for representing her brand, and the other is a disguise—to keep her identity as Rita Balman hidden beneath Carina Christien's façade. With her thick, distinct makeup, plus the colored contacts that are often paired with an eyepatch, Carina has no resemblance to Rita. Look, this is Rita minus the Carina gear." Kimmie showed her phone screen to Rick. I leaned forward and took a glimpse of the photo on the screen.

"She's blonde when she's Rita," I said, which prompted Kimmie to chuckle.

"Yes, she's naturally blonde. I often tell her it's a sacrilege, hiding her beautiful hair from the world."

On Kimmie's phone, Rita was displaying a shy smile. The facial features were on the smaller side, and just like Kimmie mentioned, the transition into Carina was quite a makeover. If Rita walked past sans makeup, I would never have recognized her as Carina Christien.

"Do you call that a disguise? Carina looks just like Rita with heavy makeup." Rick was frowning uncertainly, but he turned to Natalia. "So, can you walk me through what happened on the night of

Rita's fall?"

"Rita was totally hot for her editor, Dylan, you know. On that night, she was having fits over Dylan's shotgun marriage. Catherine and I were worried, so we went to console her. She was acting somewhat erratic. We left her condo to purchase her favorite sweets and went back. And the next thing we knew, Rita was lying injured on the patio, sporting a red ribbon around her neck." Natalia's speech was almost identical to what Catherine had told us.

Rick was listening in a relaxed manner, and as Natalia finished, a corner of his lips quirked up.

"What? Did you find any discrepancies between Catherine's and my stories?" Snorting like a mean girl from high school, Natalia defiantly crossed her arms.

"No. I found no disagreement with your story compared to Catherine's." Rick shook his head. "Thank you for taking time to speak with us. And the next person is Tyson. Will you tell him to come up?" He stood and offered his hand to her, but Natalia kept her arms crossed.

"No, thank you. I'm sick of good-looking guys who play it nice." She stood up and left.

A while after Natalia had disappeared down the stairs, other footsteps echoed and Tyson, the photographer, emerged into the café. His reluctance for the meeting was palpable as he came in yawning and slouched on the sofa without even saying hello.

"So, what do you want?" Crossing his legs, Tyson glared at Rick.

Knowing Rick, I half expected him to grab the photographer and shake him until he let slip something juicy, but he just shrugged casually. "Hey, I wasn't expecting to be dragged into this mess."

Tyson looked a little taken aback, but soon his shoulders relaxed. "Neither was I," he said, scratching his head. Then he offered the hint of a smile.

"All right, so let's make it quick. How did you get acquainted with Carina Christien?"

"Well, let me see...." Tyson looked up in the air as if he were replaying his memory. "When Carina's books took off, her publisher arranged an interview with a relatively huge magazine, and I happened to be the photographer. She loved my work, and after that she often hired me for her official website and social media."

"Was that the first time Carina sported her Goth-princess style?" Rick interjected.

"Yeah, that's right. At first, she was there without the funky makeup and Goth-princess getup, looking like the girl next door. You know, her temper's quite something, going up and down and so on. Just a split second before I clicked my camera, she started sobbing, telling me she couldn't tolerate her photos spreading across the country. Harry, my assistant, did a good job calming her down. He took her to the adjoining room, had a long chat, and then she bounced out of the room, declaring, 'Right now, I'm reborn as Carina Christien!' And thus her current style was born. In retrospect, that was one of the smartest marketing plans. Her funky-sick appearance broadened her readership and fan base. Her new style matched her books, making for great publicity."

"I see. So, as you knew both her styles of being Rita and Carina, she was comfortable working with you in terms of saving her from explaining about her alter ego every time."

"I guess." Tyson chuckled.

"Did you have a personal relationship with

Carina as well as business?"

"Nah. Everything was business." The photographer shook his head. "She often hosted post-photo-session dinners at fancy places. Carina had a crush on Harry, my assistant, and I'm guessing that's why she wanted to dine with us so often. She wasn't happy when Harry started dating Catherine," he said sarcastically.

I felt sorry for Carina. If dying from her fall was bad enough, now everyone was gossiping about her allegedly failed romances. Talk about rubbing salt on the wound! Still, Tyson's comments didn't make sense, considering Catherine and Natalia said Carina's crush was Dylan Woodhouse....

"By the way, it looks like the photos on Carina's official website change on a monthly basis. Did you take them all?" Rick asked.

"Oh, yeah. Her gung-ho fans, the Carinists, are always looking forward to seeing new photos of her, and Carina herself regarded her photos as an important tool in keeping her brand." Tyson nodded.

"Most of the photos are quite graphic, like the author soaking in a blood bath. Marilyn Manson meets Betsey Johnson," Rick commented.

"I know. Her branding strategy was lovesick girl going mentally sick. Sometimes her eccentric photos made an Internet frenzy involving the Carinists, trolls and everything. She once mentioned such flaming is a calculated process, and I was like wow! She seemed to be enjoying the attention. No such thing as bad press, I guess."

"So who drew the outline of her next photos? Carina herself?"

"Yes, she did, linking them with her latest release and sometimes the movies based on her books. Harry usually listened to her and developed detailed concepts."

"I see." Rick nodded. "So, just a moment before Carina's fall, you were talking to her on the phone. Was that conversation about the photo shoot?"

"Of course. Work is the only conversation topic I've had with her. I don't recall talking about anything else," Tyson said defiantly.

"Why did you call her twice?"

"I forgot to ask her the shooting time, so I called her back to clarify."

"I see. Can you give me the exact time and date for the agreed photo shoots?"

"What? I don't remember. If you recall, everything happened a year ago." While answering Rick's question, Tyson irritably tapped the floor with the tip of his boot.

"Okay, fine. Thanks for your cooperation. Can you tell your assistant to come up and speak with me?"

"Uh-huh." Tyson stood up and left the room. Along with his echoing footsteps down the stairs, we heard him say, "Hey, Harry, you're next. Come up and talk to that guy."

CHAPTER 6

After Tyson left, I was regurgitating his story, wondering who Carina's real love interest was. Suppose Tyson was right and she had a crush on Harry; seeing him having a relationship with one of her best friends should have been traumatizing. Still, considering that her crush was just a one-way love, Carina's pride wouldn't have allowed her to act out and let Catherine know her true feelings toward Harry. Hmm... perhaps Carina lied to Catherine and Natalia in an attempt to hide her feelings and told them she loved her editor, Dylan Woodhouse. That was possible.... Then again, if Dylan Woodhouse wasn't Carina's love interest, that meant Catherine and Natalia were lying.

Then I realized that Rick didn't seem to ask anything critical about the case. "Hey, Rick, why don't you grab every suspect and shake them until someone fesses up?"

"Because that'll spoil the whole fun of hunting the culprit," he said nonchalantly. Then he remembered the victim's sister was there. "No offense." He turned to Kimmie and winked at her.

"None taken," she replied breathlessly.

Before I had a chance to ask him about the meaning of his wink, Harry sheepishly came inside.

"Hi, Harry. Thanks for taking your time." Rick stood up and indicated to a chair instead of the sofa that time, sporting a relaxed smile. "Have a seat."

"Th-thanks." Harry nervously took a seat. He immediately began fretting, sweat beading on his forehead even though the place wasn't hot.

"So, I need to ask you some questions about your photo shoots with Carina."

Harry visibly tensed. "Ph-ph-photo shoots?" he squawked.

"Yes." Without saying anything else, Rick looked at the photographer's assistant straight in his face.

Harry gulped. "Which photo shoot?"

"The first time your boss took photos of Carina Christien."

"Oh… that time?" Harry let out a sigh. I could see he was trying his best to be discreet, but so far, he was failing miserably. He took a handkerchief out of his jacket pocket and wiped his sweaty forehead.

"I heard Carina started crying, saying she didn't want to expose her face, and you took her to have a little chat and successfully consoled her by offering a game-changing plan for her career—to create a whole new Carina Christien."

"Oh, you're talking about *that* time. Ah… memories." Harry's tense face broke into a smile.

"Your boss was very impressed with the way you persuaded her into having her photos taken. Would you care to share the trick you used on her with us?"

"The trick? No, nothing like that. I had noticed Carina carrying a Joan of Arc charm from *Clone High* strapped on her purse, and I mentioned that I was a huge fan of the series. Then she opened up and told me about her love of that series, too." Harry spoke carefully, and Rick gave occasional nods as if to encourage him to go on.

"As we chatted, I suggested creating a whole new character who had no resemblance to herself as Rita Balman, and she absolutely loved it. I drew some rough sketches of possible Carina Christien's appearance. Then I took in Carina's writing style and her tastes, and then the Carina Christien we see today was born."

"And the photos of Carina Christien on the magazine made quite a riot, right?" Rick interjected.

"Oh, yes. I was glad about the reaction." Harry flashed a wide grin.

"By the way, I heard you're dating Carina's friend, Catherine." As Rick abruptly changed the subject, Harry turned pink in the ears.

"Yes. It was love at first sight on my part. She's gorgeous, smart, and such fun to be around."

"So you approached her, asking her out, perhaps?"

Harry shook his head. "No. Actually, I couldn't. I thought she'd already be taken, and I couldn't make a move, but she talked to me often, telling me things like, 'Hey, Harry, you like me a lot, don't you?' At first, I thought she was just playing with me. Then we started going out, and…."

In my opinion, Catherine's tactics seemed clever but lewd, but observing Harry turning red, I had to admit her strategy actually worked. I took a glance at Rick, picturing myself asking him the same question… and I admired her guts.

"So, on the night of Carina's fall, Tyson phoned her. You were with him, weren't you?"

"Um, well… I guess I was with him, but my memory's a bit hazy. You know, it's been a long time… but I guess I was with him since I'm always sticking around my boss." Harry knitted his eyebrows, and he was sweating again.

"Indeed, Tyson called her not just once but twice. Do you know why?"

"That's because Tyson forgot to ask her the timing for the photo shoot. I remember my boss checking the time with her over the phone. You know, timing is everything with photo shoots. A moment's lag ruins the whole picture." Harry sounded more confident that time.

"I see." A corner of Rick's lips quirked up like he was enjoying this conversation. "I've got it. Thanks. Now can you tell Dylan Woodhouse to come upstairs?"

"I will. Nice talking to you." Standing up, Harry let out a deep sigh. When he turned on his heels to leave, Rick called to his back, "Harry, just one more question," prompting him to jump a few inches.

"Excuse me?" Gasping, Harry turned back.

"According to Tyson, Carina had a huge crush on you. Were you aware of that?"

Following Rick's bold question, Harry's jaw dropped. "Carina having a crush on me? No way, that's impossible. Besides, I've been told that Carina fancies Dylan, her former editor," he said in a serious tone.

"I see. Thanks for the info." Afterward, Harry left, shaking his head like he was truly confused.

The moment Harry was out of earshot, Rick turned to Kimmie. "Harry or Dylan. Who's your sister's true love interest? What do you think about that, Kimmie?" he asked in a low voice that was almost a whisper.

Kimmie, who was looking down at the floor, jerked her head up. "Well… I think Rita trusted Harry as a good partner, but I have a hunch Dylan was the man she truly cared for," she said hesitantly.

"Don't you talk about each other's love lives?" Rick asked.

"Rita would get bashful when discussing romantic topics. Whenever I asked her things like, 'Met any cute guys?' she would blush and say something like, 'Come on, stop interrogating me!' and dodge my questions."

"That's interesting." As Rick chuckled, Dylan Woodhouse entered the café.

"Hi," he said and took a seat across the table from Rick. "Rick, I'm sorry about this mess."

"No need for an apology. I'm blaming my old man." Rick shrugged. "Still, considering no one's gotten shot by now, I'd call this evening rather peaceful."

"Oh…." Displaying a polite but confused smile, Dylan Woodhouse let out something between a groan and an agreement.

"So, you used to be Carina's editor. Were you in charge of her since the very beginning of her career?"

Following Rick's straightforward question, Dylan shifted in his chair. "Yes."

"Can you walk me through the process of your becoming her editor? Was she just assigned to you?"

"No. The editors in the mystery section at the publishing house took a large part in selecting the winners of the contest Carina had entered. Each editor got to cast a vote on their most favorite candidate, and once the candidate won something, the editor who voted for him or her could keep on working with the author. The policy was based on the principle that an editor has to love something about a certain author's work to create the best possible work with the author."

"I see. So when the author hits the bestsellers lists, the credit directly goes to the editor, doesn't it?"

"Um… right." Dylan nodded at Rick's comment with a slight hesitation.

"Given the process of co-creating Carina Christien's bestselling books, what moved you out of the mystery section?"

"That's because…," Dylan started, but he stopped short, and after a moment of silence, he sighed. "I mean, you know Violet Huss, and your father is Daniel Rowling, so it does no good making a cover story, right?"

"I'm listening," Rick said, without answering the editor's question.

"All right. So basically, Carina wasn't happy about my recent marriage," Dylan said through gritted teeth. "She got hysterical, to the point of making it an issue involving management and HR. The company came to the conclusion that we were irreconcilable."

"So, Carina set her heart on you, but…."

"Right. At least that's what I heard. Though I thought Harry Geiser, the assistant photographer, was her love interest." Dylan shook his head. "I still remember when Harry started dating Catherine. At that time, Carina had a meltdown, shrieking that she couldn't write a word anymore. If she were one of those struggling authors, I could have just said whatever and walked away, but I was dealing with Carina Christien, whose books are constantly on multiple bestsellers lists. I worked my ass off consoling her."

"I get the picture." Rick nodded. "In the beginning, Carina had a crush on Harry, but her one-way love failed as he started seeing Catherine. She was heartbroken and desperate, but you stuck with her, comforting her, encouraging her, reminding her that she's wonderful. She recovered enough to keep writing her bestselling books, and her heart moved on to you." Rick looked straight into Dylan's eyes. Dylan shrugged helplessly. "And you were fully aware of that, weren't you?"

"I had a hunch, but I pretended not to notice her… feelings."

"Smart move." A corner of Rick's lips quirked up. "If I were you, I'd have taken the same measure."

"Thanks," Dylan mumbled.

"So, after you broke up with Carina, you're now in charge of Violet Huss."

"Except I'm only partially in charge of Violet," Dylan corrected. "I'm just a sub-editor with Violet's work. Before she had her work published, I'd made some suggestions to her about her manuscript, and she still appreciates them. That's why I still have my job at the publishing house. Considering the grim environment of publishing, quitting my job and starting over was out of the question, especially being newly married and with a baby. So, I sucked it up and accepted my transfer to the erotica section. Violet's main editor is the chief editor of that section, and I'm more like an assistant. In exchange, her former sub-editor got my position at the mystery section." He smiled weakly, but anyone could tell he wasn't in the mood for smiling.

"What a shame. You could have been the next chief editor at the mystery section," Rick said sympathetically, prompting Dylan to almost nod.

"Well… I mean, my screwy relationship doesn't make me a killer. Besides, I was in the office at the time of the incident. Even if my marriage had mentally pushed her off the balcony, that doesn't make me a killer, does it?" he said hurriedly.

"Of course not. Still, dealing with your star author's meltdown must have been upsetting, right?"

"Right. Except, in my opinion, an apocalypse sounds like a more appropriate term than a meltdown to describe those hijinks. That got me panicked, really." Dylan took a deep breath.

"So, you sought help from her friends, Catherine and Natalia, didn't you?" Rick said nonchalantly, but Dylan's eyes widened.

"How did you know that?"

"You told me they've been occasional heroes for you when you introduced them to me," Rick pointed out. "Not to mention, editors don't talk to their authors' friends that often."

"Oh… my blabbermouth. Can't hide anything from you." Dylan chuckled drily. "I met them at Carina's office and we exchanged our cards. I thought a little help from them would smoothen up things, but it didn't work."

"Now I've got the picture. So, can you call Larry Burton up?"

When Rick said that, Jackie popped up in front of my face. "Mayday, mayday! We have a major emergency! That dude who looks a little cute in a bad guy biker way, he just stormed out of the cottage!"

"Seriously?" I gasped.

"What's the matter?" Rick, who couldn't hear Jackie's voice, frowned as he took in my alarm.

"It's about Larry Burton. He's—" As I spoke, we heard someone rushing up the stairs.

Catherine burst into the café and pointed at the window. "Hey, that guy, Larry Burton? He's leaving, saying this is ridiculous."

When I glanced at the window, I saw the P.I. powerwalking out of the cottage. "He's really leaving—Rick?" Rick was already running down the stairs. Gosh, he was fast.

I was going to run after him, but I was wearing a pair of midheel pumps. I proceeded carefully so as not to fall down the stairs.

When I finally caught up with Rick, Larry Burton was already on a motorcycle with its engine revving, except the P.I. had one of his wrists captured in Rick's death grip.

"Get off me! Do you wanna get hurt?" Burton threatened, trying to shake Rick off.

"I said all you need to do is answer one question," Rick said calmly.

"And I said I can't disclose info regarding my gig with Carina Christien!" Burton shot back.

"You don't need to disclose anything. Hey, look at me." Rick stared at Burton in the eyes.

"Ha!" The P.I. snorted and glared back at his captor.

"Carina hired you for two background check cases, targeting someone attending this event, right?"

I saw Burton's shoulders slightly twitching.

"The total number of targets was three. Two for the first gig, and one for the second gig," Rick went on, and Burton gasped.

"Wh-what are you, a psychic?" he stuttered, and then he shook his arm with all his might and left. The sound of the blasting engine lingered even after the motorcycle went out of sight.

"Ohmygawd! He's gone!" Jackie exclaimed.

Kimmie, who ran out of the cottage, gasped. "Oh, did he slip out?"

I clutched Rick's jacket sleeve. "Should we go after him?"

"No need for that. At least I've covered the bases." He shrugged and turned to face the rest of the members coming out to witness the altercation. "All right, that's about it for the interviews. Now I'll tell you what happened on the night of Carina's fall. Everyone, please gather upstairs."

CHAPTER 7

Following Rick's order, we moved to the café in the upstairs of the cottage. That time, no one dared to escape.

While waiting for everyone to settle, Rick stood by the window overlooking the winter garden illuminated by mellow lighting. Leaning nonchalantly on the window frame, he was silent, looking like a model on a photo shoot for *GQ* magazine. In front of him, the people related to Carina Christien shifted and fretted uncomfortably.

It was only a short while, but the stillness seemed to last forever.

When the strain in the room reached its maximum level, Tyson opened his mouth to break the silence.

"So, let me tell you my opinion," he said before Tyson had a chance to utter a word. Everyone gulped in anticipation topped with fear.

"Have you found out the truth?" Kimmie asked breathlessly. Her voice was shaky, her anxiety palpable.

"Well, it's not that dramatic as finding the truth. I'll just be telling you my deduction based on what everyone here has told me. Unfortunately, it's just a hypothesis, and even if it turns out to be true, I don't have supporting evidence. I believe things will be different when it gets upgraded into an open investigation of a homicide, with the police, CSI, and everything."

"A theory is good enough. Will you, please?" Kimmie stared at Rick with intense eyes.

"Fine. Kimmie, I have one thing to clarify with you. What was written in your sister's alleged suicide note?" Rick stared back at Kimmie, prompting her to quiver.

She opened her mouth, but she stopped short of starting a sentence.

Rick spoke for her. "Carina didn't want to make that suicide note public, and that's why she avoided having her fall investigated as a murder—no, an attempted murder back then—right?"

Kimmie looked past him for a moment, and then she gave him a resigned smile.

"The suicide note was a confession, wasn't it? And that made you believe your sister attempted to kill herself."

I wasn't quite following what Rick was saying, but Kimmie nodded and let out a small sigh. "Yes, it was. Gosh, I can't hide anything from you, can I?"

"Can you recite the sentences written in your sister's note?" Rick pressed on.

"It started by saying, 'I, Carina Christien, am confessing to deceiving my readers,' and the note went so far as to state that she didn't write any of her bestselling books by herself," Kimmie said through gritted teeth.

"What do you think about the contents of this note, Kimmie?"

"I felt that was a downright lie. I've seen my sister working hard on her stories every day for years! How can I believe such nonsense?"

"Hmm… in that case, what made your sister so reluctant to report an attempted murder to the police?" Rick went on. "Because there was a sliver of truth contained in the alleged suicide note."

"No," Kimmie muttered, but she couldn't go on. Fat tears rolled down her cheeks.

"Anyway, I'm sure that not everything written was the truth. Perhaps a half-truth covered with lies to be presentable, or rather two-thirds of the truth covered with another third of lies."

"Two-thirds of the truth? What do you mean?" I muttered without thinking, totally clueless.

Rick flashed his perfect set of pearly whites. "I'm talking about the pen name, Carina Christien. It was originally created by Catherine Davenport, Rita Balman, and Natalia Rain—three girls who loved Agatha Christie mysteries—wasn't it?" he declared without the slightest hint of hesitation, and my eyes widened. "Though Carina Christien's writing style has its own distinctness, I noticed her fondness and homage toward Agatha Christie, the queen of British crime novels, when I read her books. I had a hunch that the surname Christien evolved from Christie. The information about Carina's real name being Rita Balman and the names of her friends being Catherine Davenport and Natalia Rain was the dead giveaway. All of them have an N in their surname, and that's why it had to be Christien instead of Christie. Also, Carina is the combination of the first syllable of each girl's first name. It could have been Narica, Canari, Ricana, or Rinaca, except Carina sounds more natural than the other names."

"Wow, Carina Christien used to be a writing group rather than a person," I muttered.

"At least that's what I presume." Rick glanced at Catherine and Natalia, who were silent, blanched, and frozen, as if someone turned them into stone.

Their reaction seemed to be the telltale sign that he was correct.

"Now let me tell you my opinion based on this presumption about the origin of the pen name Carina Christien," he said breezily. "Three girls from the same high school were volunteering at a local library. One day, it was discovered that Rita was writing a novel, so Catherine and Natalia took on writing as well. Still, everyone was lacking something from their work. Rita could write, but her story didn't have the climax or catharsis. Catherine's characters were passable, but her writing itself was disastrous. And Natalia could plot, but she loathed writing. The lightbulb moment was when they recognized each other's strengths and weaknesses. At that moment, no one could write solo, but what if they wrote as a trio?"

Rick eyed Catherine and Natalia, as if to check out his theory, but they were silent and averted their gazes.

"Considering that Rita was the one who could write, she served as the main author while Catherine and Natalia made suggestions for character development and plotting. Perhaps their joint work turned out to be brilliant. Maybe they kept on writing and coauthored multiple stories. However, their happy writing days had to end as they graduated from high school and went separate ways. Catherine and Natalia, who weren't much into writing in the first place, moved on with their lives unrelated to writing, but Rita kept on.

"When Catherine and Natalia were in their sophomore year at college, Rita came back to their hometown for a reunion, and on that special occasion she brought up the topic of writing, which was her dream. Perhaps she asked for your permission to submit the revised version of the story which was originally done with you two. I believe Rita was serious about this submission, but you two gave her the greenlight breezily because one, neither of you was interested in writing anymore, and two, you didn't expect that your friend would actually win the contest. Anyway, after obtaining the much-needed permission from you two, Rita submitted her story under her pen name Carina Christien in a way of acknowledging and thanking her friends' contribution. Beating the odds, she won second place and a thousand bucks. She offered to treat you, but you two declined, saying, 'Thanks but no thanks. Use the money for yourself.' What a beautiful friendship! Except at that time, none of you were expecting your friend Rita Balman to become such a celebrated author."

As Rick went on, I caught Natalia frowning and Catherine exhaling deeply.

"The friendship between the three women started to distort as Rita's writing career as Carina Christien skyrocketed. Perhaps the beginning of Carina Christien was like a continued fun of their youth for Catherine and Natalia. They must have been happy to see the characters and story development they'd contributed to gain popularity. I also presume that Rita was simply grateful to her friends. Still, the sweet times didn't last forever. They might have asked Rita things like, 'Can you buy that for me?' 'I wish I could rent that pretty apartment in Chelsea,' and 'You're picking up the dinner tab, aren't you?'

"After college, Catherine got a job in New York and moved to the East Coast, followed by Natalia moving to the neighborhood. From the outside, it would have looked like a heartwarming episode, but it could be interpreted as emotional blackmailing from Rita's perspective. Presumably, she endured endless demands wrapped in seemingly benevolent words from her so-called friends, fooling herself into thinking that it was better than a nasty court battle. Talk about beautiful friendships turning sour. Anyway, Rita went on being treated like a doormat without taking countermeasures such as lawyering up. Still, everyone has their limit, and in her case, the last straw was witnessing Harry, her secret romantic interest, hooking up with Catherine."

Harry took a sharp intake of breath and glanced at Catherine, who bit her lower lip uncomfortably.

Rick gave a satisfied glance at the couple and went on. "Rita, totally fed up with being screwed anymore, decided to strike back. She hired Larry Burton, a P.I., to run background checks on her pals in hopes of getting even by digging up their dirty laundry. I assume from the consequences that she got ahold of the dark side of their pasts. I have no idea what Catherine's and Natalia's secrets were. Maybe Catherine had done something stupid in her happy youth, and Natalia wanted to hide the reason why she quit her old job and ran away from her hometown."

"That's enough," Natalia muttered through her gritted teeth. "Oh, yes. I was young and stupid. What's wrong with that?" She glared at Rick, who responded with a shrug.

"Hey." Catherine pulled her friend's sleeve in alarm, but that didn't stop Natalia.

Shaking off Catherine's hand, she spat, "It's no use giving my heart and soul to protect my past. You've already heard about it from that Burton guy, haven't you? Okay, so I got fired from my previous job for *borrowing* my client's money because my ex-boyfriend needed some cash desperately. And yeah, it turned out that I was conned in the first place. Luckily, my employer was generous enough to avoid pressing charges on me, but people talked, and I couldn't stay where I was. I'm not proud of my past, and Rita found out about it, going on like, 'Stop taking advantage of me. By the way, I've cancelled your apartment lease and you have two weeks to move out.' I was shocked and annoyed. Was she so superior, owing her success to us? Besides, I never demanded anything from her. She voluntarily arranged Catherine's and my apartments when we moved from the West Coast."

"That's so true!" Catherine chimed in. "Rita dug up silly stuff, like I used to have sugar daddies back in college, and I was sleeping with my boss who happened to have a wife at my former workplace. And she talked like we'd been sponging off her. We didn't like her attitude, but we didn't kill her!"

Seeing Catherine blurting out her not-so-nice past, I felt like she was using her desperation to avoid being named as the killer.

"I get your point, and I can imagine the frustration the two of you went through. After all, you appreciated Rita's wealth, but you had no intention of blackmailing her," Rick said. "Then again, Rita had been stressed out, and I can't help noticing a deep emotional river between her and the two of you."

Natalia opened her mouth like she wanted to protest, but instead she harrumphed and shut it again.

"Anyway, Rita was heartbroken. She had success, but the relationship with her old friends got screwy and the guy she really liked was swept away by one of her friends. The situation might have seemed like the end of the world to Rita, so she started grumbling about how she couldn't write anymore, and perhaps she could have gone so far as quitting being Carina Christien. Then voila! A knight in shining armor appeared in front of her." Rick turned to Dylan Woodhouse. "And it was you, Dylan."

"Well, a knight in shining armor sounds like a stretch," Woodhouse mumbled.

"You worked your ass off consoling and encouraging the heartbroken author. Of course, that's the right thing to do, considering an author who sells millions of copies without breaking a sweat is hard to come across." Rick winked. "Anyway, you had a natural way with ladies, and I'm guessing you used your charm to steer Rita into loving you. Promising words and actions that implied you genuinely cared for her should have done the trick. Thanks to your hard work, Carina Christien kept on writing her bestselling books. You worked very hard at keeping secret the fact that you had a steady girlfriend, didn't you? You intended to keep the existence of your girlfriend from your star author for a while, at least until getting promoted to chief editor."

Rick gave Dylan a sideways glance.

"Dylan, I guess you underestimated the woman's instinct. Perhaps Carina had a gut feeling that you'd been hiding something from her. So again she hired Larry Burton, who found out about your very steady girlfriend. And things were screwed all over again. Carina refused to pay Burton for his service, insisting she didn't believe him, and she had another temper tantrum. Meanwhile, it turned out that your girlfriend was pregnant and you were tying the knot with her, adding fuel to Carina's anger. As a result, the trouble between you and her got out of control, spreading to the publisher as well. In a desperate attempt for damage control, you sought help from Carina's best friends—at least, you regarded Catherine and Natalia as her best friends. Anyway, when you had a talk with said friends, you learned that Carina Christien wasn't a one-woman operation by Rita Balman."

Rick spoke like he'd witnessed the whole thing, and like always, I didn't know where his confidence came from. Still, I could tell his story was mostly accurate. Catherine, Natalia, and Dylan blanched as if on cue. As for Dylan, his mouth was agape, and he didn't seem to notice. Perhaps he wouldn't have noticed if a giant frog leaped inside.

"Learning about the presence of the co-creators of meticulously developed stories and attention-grabbing characters by Carina Christien must have been a shocker. Still, this little piece of information could have helped you think about the next step—or rather a truly sinister, diabolical plan." Rick snorted.

"A diabolical plan?" Puzzled, I glanced at him.

"Oh yes, the plan goes like this: Carina Christien kills herself, confessing that it wasn't she who had been writing her bestselling books but her ghostwriters, and then the ghostwriters come into the spotlight like shooting stars. Who wouldn't be interested? Of course, as Kimmie said, Carina had no intention of killing herself. Still, she had to die to accomplish this diabolical plan. So basically, staging Carina's *suicide* to kill her was an absolutely needed process, followed by the rise of Carina's ghostwriters.

Talk about a cold-blooded scheme!"

As he went on, everyone froze in silence. It seemed like time had stopped, but Harry Geiser, the assistant photographer, held his head in his hands and started to shiver.

"Harry, I suppose you suck at lying, but I've got a hunch that you took a major part in shaping the scheme of getting rid of Rita. Perhaps Catherine steered you into coming up with the perfect scenario. Anyway, the fact that you were the mastermind of the portraits featured on Carina's website came in handy. You agreed to set death by hanging as the theme of that photo session."

Harry's face turned white like tofu.

"The plan was to lure Rita out to the balcony by convincing her to use the moonlit sky as the backdrop. Conveniently, Catherine and Natalia visited Rita's office on that special night. Maybe they acted like they wanted to make up with her. They helped you set up for the photo shoot, preparing the suicide note, too. Then the two *friends* left, or pretended to leave, with you, except either Catherine or Natalia was lurking. Meanwhile, you and Tyson began getting ready for the photo op outside of the building. By the way, both of you said the reason for making two phone calls to Rita was to settle the time for the photo shoots. Then again, neither of you gave me the exact time and date. Like I told you in the beginning, I'm just guessing, but I have a hunch that you didn't want to disclose the settled timing because the two of you were witnessing Rita's fall from outside."

Tyson cleared his throat. "For the record, I had no clue about the jeopardy my client was facing. I'm a regular photographer specializing in commercial photos, and I believed it was going to be another gig for her website, just like usual."

Rick raised an eyebrow. "Okay, so you made the first call to Rita, telling her to come out to the balcony as you were ready. When you saw her on the balcony, you called her again, telling her to climb up on the railing."

Tyson gulped. "Yeah, right. She followed my instructions and climbed up on the railing. Dressed in black, sporting red shoes and a red ribbon around her neck. I was in the zone, shooting my camera at her like a maniac, just like usual."

"Except either Catherine or Natalia came out from hiding and pushed Rita off the rail." Rick went on, looking Tyson straight in the eyes. "You witnessed Rita falling, yet you decided to keep your mouth shut. I don't know the reason why and I don't care."

Tyson opened his mouth to say something, but words failed to come.

Rick crossed his arms. "Anyway, Catherine, Natalia, Dylan, Tyson, and Harry—all of you were either directly or indirectly involved with the murder of Rita Balman. The turn of events reminds me of the Agatha Christie mysteries, except this is no entertainment. Still, as I told you in the beginning, all I have is theory, and I have no evidence. Perhaps if Rita was alive and she recalled what happened on that night, things would change." Then he turned to Kimmie. "That's about it. Are you happy now, *Rita*?"

When he said the name, everyone gasped, and I cocked my head to the side, wondering if he'd confused the sisters' names. Kimmie took a sharp intake of breath and reached for the choker necklace.

"The red stone on Kimmie's necklace is a

hidden camera available for $240.99 at USCAB's online store." Rick pointed at her necklace. "I have a hunch that Rita's been watching us from somewhere close by."

"B-but… isn't she supposed to be… dead?" When Dylan stuttered, the sound of heels clicking on the hardwood echoed from the stairs.

The sound ceased when she entered the café.

She was dressed in a black dress and black coat with lots of frills and ribbons, topped with a black lacey veil covering her face a la funeral style. If it were a photograph, she might have looked like the portrait of a woman in a black-and-white photo, except the ribbon wrapped around her neck and her platform heels were the color of blood spewing from the aorta.

When she lifted the veil, exposing her face, I gasped. Her alabaster skin was flawless, her lips were crimson, and her eyes looked huge as they were surrounded by cobwebs drawn in black eyeliner. But the most striking part was her pupils because they were red, as if she were bleeding from both eyes. I knew she was sporting red contact lenses. Still, seeing a woman with crimson pupils was scary.

Emerging from the stairs in her full Carina Christien gear, Rita looked at everyone's face with her crimson eyes.

"Hello, everyone. I'm finally back from my deathbed. Nice seeing you again!" She was smiling, and the tone of her voice was chipper, but somehow, her flamboyance made me shiver.

CHAPTER 8

Everyone except for Rick, Kimmie, and Rita froze in silence.

Rita was the one who broke it.

"Hello, Rick. I'm so very much impressed with your deduction." She moved her gaze to him and offered a content smile. "Actually, you've definitely surpassed my expectations."

"Glad I could help." He chuckled wryly. "I knew you were alive."

"How did you know that, if I may ask?" Rita tilted her head to the side.

"Aside from your sister's necklace being a dead giveaway?" He shrugged. "First of all, since you'd been plotting this for over a month, your alleged death was too sudden. Not to mention your sister was too well-composed considering that she's supposed to have lost her sister who meant more than her parents. Besides, it wouldn't be easy to keep the media from having a field day about your mysterious death, in case you were actually dead. And one more thing. The part about you having no memory of the night of your attempted murder isn't true."

As he looked her directly in the eyes, Rita's lips parted, showing beautiful yet slightly unnaturally white teeth. Watching the teeth gleaming, I assumed that she'd had a dental job while recovering from the injuries.

"You're right. I've been lying to Kimmie. When I climbed up the railing, Catherine came out to the balcony, and then she pushed me off to the condo's patio. I remember that," she said matter-of-factly.

"What?" Kimmie gasped. "If you remember that, why did you take such a measure? We should have pressed charges against her!"

Facing a confused glare by her sister, Rita let out a small sigh. "Sorry about lying to you, Kimmie, but I was literally dying to know why Catherine tried to kill me. Okay, so I knew she felt bitter about me. Then again, her decision-making process is completely based on the calculation of pros and cons, so I'd been thinking what she'd obtain by killing me off. In the meantime, when I was recovering from the injuries, Dan Rowling caught wind of my *accident,* and he kindly paid me a visit."

Rick's eyebrows visibly twitched the moment his dad's name was mentioned.

"I was surprised at first. After all, we'd met just a few times when he helped me with my research. Dan has been so warm, kind, and supportive, listening as I sobbed my heart out to him. When I finished crying, he said he had a hunch that his son would be able to help me disentangle the situation."

Rick slapped his forehead with the palm of his hand, muttering, "I didn't know that guy's been helping this many authors with their research."

Rita's face turned solemn. "I know it's egoistic of me to drag you into this mess of mine, but I was desperate to know the reason why it happened, so I couldn't say no to his kind offer. He said this setting was perfect, and I can't agree more. Look, Rick, I know you were not keen on coming here at all. I apologize for all this trouble, and again, thank you so much."

Then she took a deep bow.

"No need for an apology. The fault is all his... I mean, my old man's the one who organized everything... including but not limited to that double-date with Violet Huss." Clenching his hands into fists, Rick smiled tightly, except his eyes were not smiling. Dan was in trouble.

He then took a deep breath to pull himself together. "So Rita, now that you know everything, what's your next step?"

"Well, for starters...." Rita smirked and slipped her hand into the pocket of her coat.

"No!"

Everyone gasped when her hand reappeared, holding a gun and aiming it at them.

The problem was I was sitting near her enemies and there was the possibility of getting hurt, or worse. Suddenly, I was swiped off my chair as I froze there with my mouth agape like an idiot.

"Rick!" I gasped. After setting me down, he stood in front of me, shielding me with his body.

"It's okay," he whispered, his eyes focusing on Rita. "Just stay calm."

I reached for his hand, and when he held mine back, I almost cried.

"Hey, Rita, you can't shoot me!" Dylan snapped. Rita's gun was trained at him.

"You think so? Let's see if you're right— though it may turn out you're dead wrong." Rita chuckled. "Having cut off my ties with my friends, thanks to your deception, I was totally devastated and toyed with the idea of killing myself. My favorite weapon for committing suicide is a gun. An easy getaway is one of the perks of death by gun, but you can't ignore how red blood looks stunning in contrast to a black gun. Oh, did I mention that your scheme of trying to kill me by hanging grossed me out? Why should I die in such a gruesome way? No thanks, no siree. I'll paint you all red with a trick of bullets. Don't worry. When I've taken care of you all, I'll join you in hell."

Catherine shrieked. "Hey, Rick! You have to do something to help us! Detain her or something. You're supposed to serve and protect us people!"

"I don't think so." Rick shrugged. "I'm off duty today, and I'm not packing heat. Considering that she's got no reason to hurt me or my partner here, I don't wanna become collateral damage by trying to be a hero. Besides, I have a dinner reservation I don't want to miss by injuring myself."

My ears perked up when I caught the phrase "my partner." "Rick, did you just say—"

He quickly shushed me, prompting me to shut up.

"So Dylan, answer my question carefully. You lie a little, and I'll shoot you. You're the one who plotted and planned the whole thing, right?" Rita asked in a cold tone with her gun trained on Dylan's chest.

"Oh yeah! The hell I did! I thought my plan would be a riot for publicity, and I was tempted to shape a legendary bestsclling author who came back out of the ruin like a fucking phoenix! Still, I'm not the one who committed an actual murder attempt. She's the one who pushed you!" Spewing saliva from the corner of his mouth, Dylan pointed his accusing finger at Catherine.

"Hello? You're the one who brainwashed me into committing that terrible crime!" Catherine shot back at Dylan, and then she turned to Rita. "Look,

Rita, I'm so sorry! I just had temporary insanity. Just like he conned you, he conned me, too. Please forgive me. I'm really glad you've recovered."

"You've been conned? What? Are you trying to put all the blame on me? Y-you're the one who started it!"

As Dylan's voice rose an octave, Rita snorted disgustedly. "I don't care about who started this mess. I'm so shocked to have learned that you decided to kill someone for such a trivial reason. By the way, Catherine, you have to take everything from me, don't you? You used to be uninterested in Harry, but the moment you noticed that I liked him a lot, you suddenly developed a huge crush on him. Hey, Catherine, you're obsessed with taking everything from someone else, aren't you? I know you slept with Dylan, too. Don't even think about lying to me or else I'll shoot you first."

"Aargh!" Catherine wailed. "You're right! I got interested in Harry because you said you cared for him, and I slept with Dylan! But you've got everything, so I figured you wouldn't care. On the contrary, I have no potential for success and I know it! My looks are ordinary, and I'm not talented like you. You know I was jealous of you! I was envious of your accomplishments! I ended up having this silly misbelief that I could prove I'm greater than you if I got the hearts of the men you couldn't win. I'm sorry!" She threw herself on the floor and cried, begging for mercy.

Natalia stood by Catherine's side. "I will not apologize to you!" she snapped. "Okay, so I admit to having taken your generosity for granted, just like Catherine did. Then again, if you hated our guts so much, you could have just told us so. Instead of communicating with us, you hired that Burton person, having him snooping around us and digging into my past that I wasn't proud of. That's… that's outrageous! Guess what? I wanted to kill you. So, go ahead, kill me already if you want to. I've toyed with the idea of killing myself anyway!"

Unlike her friend, Natalia sounded oh-so-defiant, but I had a hunch that her attitude was merely a façade. The sense of self-importance about her was apparent from her past words and attitude.

Perhaps Rita was aware of Natalia's thought patterns. She responded by raising one corner of her crimson lips.

All of a sudden, Harry scurried toward Rita and knelt on the floor.

"Rita, I'm so sorry for everything that happened!" he apologized profusely, prompting Rita to frown, still holding the gun in her hand.

"I wasn't aware of your feelings. Though I always liked you more than my boss's client, I had this fixation that our relationship should be solely based on business. I'm merely an assistant photographer and you're Carina Christien. Anyone can see that I'm no match to you, so I forced myself to hide my feelings toward you for the fear of becoming a laughingstock. Then I met Catherine at your office… and I fell for her. Having no idea that everything was a calculated ploy, I fell really hard for her. In retrospect, I can't believe my stupidity, but it's also true that I played a crucial part in the whole mess." His eyes were brimming with tears as he spoke.

He seemed like a good guy, except maybe a tad bit dense in the romance department.

"This is all my fault, and I should be the one

to take all the blame. On top of it all, you've suffered enough, and those people are not worth killing by yourself!"

One moment he was making a tearful confession, and then he jumped up and snatched the gun out of Rita's hand.

"Harry, no!" Tyson yelled while Catherine, Natalia, Dylan, and I gasped.

Without the slightest hint of hesitation, Harry put the muzzle of the gun to his temple and pulled the trigger. The gunshot sound was inaudible, but blood splattered on the right side of his face.

"Wahhhhh!" I screamed along with everyone else, while Jackie shrieked by my ear at the top of her lungs.

"Ohmygawd, Ohmygawd, Ohmygawd!" Despite being dead herself, Jackie was shivering and blanched. "Ohmygawd! I can't believe I just witnessed a suicide! Guess what? This is turning out to be the worst Christmas ever!" She added, "Okay, my first Christmas since my death was just as terrible, so I guess it's a tie."

"Jackie, you can go back to the chicken-eating Christmas party. Guess what? My situation is far worse. Now that Harry's dead, the police will be involved and we're likely to spend the rest of the evening answering their questions! Talk about a ruined Christmas!" I hissed, totally forgetting that the presence of the ghost was supposed to be a secret.

I saw Rick's shoulders shaking. Perhaps he was angry at himself for not being able to save Harry from himself.

Then Harry cocked his head to the side and touched the temple he'd just shot, muttering, "What's wrong? Why doesn't it hurt at all? All I felt was a slight coldness."

Harry took a whiff of his hand smeared in red and gasped, "Man, it's ketchup!"

Rick was practically laughing his ass off. "Bravo! Thanks for the great entertainment." He whistled, clapping his hands. "By the way, the gun's not real. That's a toy."

I clutched Rick's arm, coming out of hiding behind his back. "Did you know it was a toy?"

"Yup. The most thrilling part was wondering when Harry would realize he's holding a toy gun," he replied, still chuckling.

"Rick, you should have told us!" Jackie pouted. I nudged Rick, repeating what she said.

Rita stood still for a moment, like she was completely taken aback by Harry's abrupt reaction. But it didn't take long for her to regain her composure.

She let out a small sigh, then smirked. "Oh yes, Rick's right. The gun was just a toy, but it did an excellent job drawing confessions from all of you. By the way, the entire conversation has been recorded, and I've kept my office preserved since the night of my attempted murder. It's a crime scene with evidence. I'll think about my next step, whether to file charges on you or not.

"Anyway, enjoy your lives dreading when you'll be arrested. That's about it for now. You can leave." Snatching the toy gun from Harry's hand, Rita indicated to the exit with the barrel.

With various expressions of fear, annoyance, and panic mixed all into one, the participants of the night's reading hurried toward the stairs.

As the stomping footsteps lingered on, Rita, Kimmie, Rick, and I remained in the café.

No one said a word until the footsteps were no longer heard.

Rita was staring at the window with a sad expression. Despite being in full Carina Christien gear, she didn't resemble the star author I'd seen in the media. After what seemed like forever, she muttered, "Gosh, I feel so empty. I finally had closure, but I still don't know why I survived. It could have been easier if I—"

"Hey, people die when they die," Rick interrupted. "You survived because you weren't meant to die last Christmas."

Rita's eyes widened.

"You can spend the rest of your life pitying yourself for the terrible incident, but at the same time, you can work your magic, turning it into one of your great works of literature. It's up to you. Still, if I'm to speak as your follower, I'm looking forward to reading more of your work."

"My follower?" Rita frowned. "You heard that neither the characters nor the plotlines of my early work were mine."

"So what? The plotlines and characters themselves can't be presented to the public without the well-structured sentences that compel the readers to go on with the story. You know what? Everyone's got an interesting story or two, but most people spend their lives without selling them. The biggest reason for that is because they don't write them at all, and even if they started writing, the majority quit before finishing them. I found your writing style quite fascinating, the meticulous structure and the process of the mystery and tragedy settling beautifully."

"Rick…." Rita took a sharp intake of air.

"Every bit of your life has the potential to

become the motivation for your work as a creator—which is the phrase my acquaintance, who happens to be a screenwriter, keeps saying. And I have a hunch that this catastrophic, yet extraordinary, experience you've gone through will take you to a whole new level," he went on, carefully observing Rita but offering a hint of a smile.

The expression on Rita's face was still tight, but it somehow softened following his words.

After a brief pause, she pressed her hand to her heart and said, "You're right, Rick. I'm no longer the same mousy girl called Rita Balman. I feel like I've finally become Carina Christien. And I promise to play God with my work and deliver my magic."

When she raised her chin with a cocky grin, she transformed into the mysterious and confident Carina Christien.

"Cool. I'm looking forward to your upcoming books." Rick nodded encouragingly, took my arm, and we left.

EPILOGUE

After parting from Carina and Kimmie, Rick and I went to the room Dan had booked for us. Technically, a suite was the more accurate term. We were in the spacious living and dining room embellished with a large, gorgeous Christmas tree, spectacular furniture, and a ton of mistletoe.

The moment we arrived at the suite, dinner was served by the butler. The food should have been superb, except my palate seemed to be taking a temporary leave. I could see only one door that would lead to a bedroom, and my heart was flip-flopping with anticipation and excitement topped with a hefty amount of panic.

Following the dessert, Rick let the butler leave. Then we were alone, sitting side by side on the sofa, enjoying a companionable silence; not even Jackie was there to disturb us. On our way from the cottage to the hotel's main building, Rick specifically asked the ghost to give us alone time for the night.

"Enjoy the night! Have a very merry and possibly superkinky Christmas!" was Jackie's reply. Then she disappeared into the night, waving with a drumstick and saying, "It's about time for the cake to be served."

Being an adult, I could imagine what was going to happen between Rick and me, and I was growing nervous, bordering on panicky. Not that I was unhappy about the prospects of sleeping with him, but….

"By the way, Rick, I didn't know you had a screenwriter friend," I said, partly to ease my nerves.

"That's because I don't have such a friend." He shrugged. Unlike me, he seemed to be at ease.

"But… what you told Carina, about utilizing every bit of her experience to create her next great work, that was so impressive and empowering."

"Good." The corner of his lips quirked into a grin. "I just made that part up. She seemed in need of a serious boost in her confidence."

"That's so sweet of you, though a tad bit uncharacteristic," I said playfully.

"Come on, I'm always sweet and nice."

I noticed Rick was looking ridiculously handsome, dressed in a dark suit, his brown hair styled in a conservatively messy 'do, and his face lit up.

"Speaking of sweet and nice, I've got a little something for you." He took out a small jewelry box from his jacket pocket. "Though we have a few hours left until twelve o'clock, here's an early Christmas gift for you. I'd say having no crazy aunts fussing about the time is one of the perks of being a grown-up."

"Right. I've brought my Christmas gift for you, too." I stood up, scurried to my rolling suitcase, and took out the bag full of assorted gifts for him. It was difficult to choose gifts for him, considering that Rick could buy most things in the world that money can buy, but still I tried. "Not that I'm complaining, but I was expecting a teddy bear," I said as I came back to the sofa.

"That was a decoy for a surprise." He smiled. "Are you ready? Okay, let's open our gifts on the count of three. One, two, three!"

Then we opened the gifts, and—

"Wow! The world's smallest walkie-talkie set? If I put on these shades, I can start a new career with the CIA anytime," Rick joked lightheartedly while he examined the assorted gifts. "And I love the cufflinks. Thanks."

When I took a glance at the item in the little box, my jaw dropped. It was the ring with pink sapphires in a four-leaf clover—the one I lost the bidding on at the charity auction. My heart stopped beating for a moment.

"Mandy?" He looked into my face as I froze in shock.

After a long pause, I opened my mouth. "Look, Rick, this is beautiful... but—"

"But what?" He furrowed his eyebrows.

"I... I... I don't know.... You know this is expensive. Too expensive to give to your assistant as a Christmas gift."

"Come on, forget about the price. The money was spent for a good cause." He shrugged.

"Excuse me? Did you outbid me at the auction?" I gasped. "That's why you left the seat during the bidding? How did you know that I made a bid in the first place?"

"I knew you wanted this when I saw your face sink during the auction. So, I started bidding until I won. Hey, Mandy, I can't just go back to them to return this ring," he replied casually and wiggled his fingers.

"Come on, Mandy! Stop grumbling and just accept the ring! All you need to do is thank him!" Jackie, who had previously promised to give us privacy, demanded, popping by my side from out of nowhere.

"She's right. Mandy. You should accept it," Giselle McCambridge, the ghost of an elderly socialite I'd met on a case, agreed, apparently tagging along with Jackie. As she pointed her finger at me, the ghost of an elderly gentleman in a black tux— Giselle's husband, I presumed—appeared by her side, smiling and patting her shoulder.

"Or else we'll bother you all night!" Jackie and Giselle threatened me in unison.

"Mandy, please don't ruin my night," Jackie said. "Like I said, I've got a hot date." As she snapped her fingers, another ghost—a cute guy in a leather jumpsuit—popped up from out of nowhere, linking his fingers with hers.

I was compelled to roll my eyes, but I put on a smile instead and said, "Okay. Thank you so much for your thoughts and, of course, the ring. This is the most beautiful ring I've ever seen. I love, love, love it!"

Rick exhaled slowly, like he was genuinely relieved. "I'm glad you like it." He took the ring out of the box and slipped it onto my left ring finger.

"Wow, the fitting's perfect," I murmured.

"That's because I measured your finger while you were asleep and had a jeweler adjust its size," he said.

"Really?" I chuckled.

"Really." He smiled widely, showing off his pearly whites. "And here's one more thing… I love you," he said, holding my hands in his.

My heart stopped beating for a second, but the next thing I knew, I was replying, "I love you, too." As I said that, I couldn't believe that it came out of me so easily. After months of pondering with no success, I was starting to suspect that I'd need some kind of life-or-death situation to actually say the big L-word.

"Sweet. I like that." He pulled me close to him. "Good thing I asked housekeeping to decorate this room with a ton of mistletoe." And then he kissed me.

I saw the quartet of ghosts cheering me on from the corner of the room. They had the audacity to snoop on my privacy, but at the same time the decency to keep their distance from me.

I shut my eyes and accepted Rick's kiss— because the tradition says a woman can't say no to a kiss when she's under the mistletoe.

About the author

Hi! My name is Lotta Smith. I'm the author of Paranormal in Manhattan Mysteries and Kelly Kinki Mysteries. I love everything comedy, from novels, TVs, to movies. In my teenage days, I was addicted to mysteries that involves amateur sleuth duo of a hot male professor and a quirky female student—with a light touch of romance sprinkled on top. So I went to medical school, partly because I wanted to see *real* dead bodies, and mostly because I was determined to meet sexy professors (specializing forensic pathology, perhaps) and go a-sleuthin'.

I got to see dead bodies and learn about the danger of petting zoos (sometimes, kids have their lips bitten off by…say, a pony!) but unfortunately, sexy professors were absolutely nonexistent. Recently, I realized that I'm a hopeless *un*romantic.

I'm hard at work writing new books.

To hear about new books and discounted book sales, please sign up for my newsletter at:
http://eepurl.com/bOSLYj
And follow me on http://amzn.to/22h0TSf

Books by Lotta Smith

Paranormal in Manhattan Mysteries:
Book 1: Wicked for Hire: http://amzn.to/25IHH6X
Sometimes, the opportunity of a lifetime busts your door instead of gently knocking at it...
FREE on Kindle Unlimited!
Medical student Amanda Meyer thought she had her life all planned out until people started dying the moment they touched her. Being cleared of any wrongdoing didn't stop the medical school from expelling her, and it didn't rid her of the unfortunate nickname Grim Reaper.
Luckily, having a rep as the harbinger of death isn't a total resume killer. Rick Rowling, Special Agent for the FBI's Paranormal Cases Division recruits her to work for the Bureau. But the sexy, brilliant, outrageous loose cannon proves to be just as untouchable as the mysterious creature or creatures that may be responsible for the seemingly unsolvable murder that becomes their first case together.
Instead of treating patients, Amanda's life becomes a test of her patience and a wild ride into the wicked paranormal world where her new boss runs the show. Together they face a ghoulish force that could destroy the entire city and a grueling family dinner that could leave Amanda contemplating harakiri.
It's a battle of life and debt [student debt, that is] and saving the world has never been so funny.

Prologue
966 Park Avenue Tower
11:48 AM, November 10…

With a weird moan, her whole body shivering, she collapses onto the sofa.

I think she's lucky that she's already sitting on the sofa as she crumples. If she was standing, she might have cracked her head on the marble floor like Humpty Dumpty—which won't be pretty.

She's lying there, totally motionless. One elbow's stiffly bent at a right angle, as if she's turned into stone as the result of looking Medusa in the eye.

I gasp—fearing she's dead.

Rick Rowling, the head of the FBI's New York Paranormal Division and my boss for the past two days, approaches and touches her neck. Looking totally blasé, he confirms that she's still alive.

I let out a sigh of relief.

On the other hand, Rowling announces that we leave the place because *"It's boring."*

My eyes widen with a total disbelief.

Of course, I disagree with him, but he brushes off my objection, stating that he doesn't care about all the crap of making arrests, prosecuting, and taking cases to trial. Again, he says that it's just a minor issue and he's way too busy for that. "You know what? I have better things to do," Rowling declares, turning on his heels to leave the condo.

"Excuse me, Rick," I call to his back.

"What?" he asks, without turning around.

"We can't just leave," I say. Then it suddenly occurs to me that offending my boss isn't in my best interest, so I add, "I'm afraid."

"Why not?" He cocks his head. "Mandy, don't be such a killjoy. The NYPD can work on the boring stuff, such as deciphering the social pathology of crimes and so on, because they have time to kill. On the other hand, I have no time to waste."

"Okay, so we don't need to decipher the social pathology of crimes, but we do need to figure out the whereabouts of the human-eating monster, don't we?" I point out.

I'm not joking or exaggerating.

I'm talking about a practically imperishable ghoul which could eat up the entire population of New York State, if not the whole world.

* * *

At precisely 2:13 in the morning, John Sangenis was standing in front of a shabby five-story apartment in Washington Heights. Fortunately, he didn't live there. He was just visiting Ivan Flynn, the insufferable asshole.

Usually, he had better things to do than visiting his worst enemy before the crack of dawn, such as sleeping like a log. Or making love with Ruth, which was even better than sleeping on his own. Ruth MacMahon was his girlfriend, who was unbelievably beautiful, dazzling, and had a truly big heart. Also, it didn't hurt that she was rich. What was more wonderful about her was she appreciated John's talent as an actor. It was a rare trait to come across in society, and it was why she happily provided him both moral and financial support.

If there were any shortcomings about her, it was that she was two-timing him with Ivan.

He thought about her taste in men, or lack thereof, and shrugged.

John wasn't the sharpest knife in the kitchen, so he didn't realize describing Ruth's taste in men as horrible was the same as admitting that he was a total loser.

A cold, wet late-autumn breeze was blowing from the East River. A sprinkle of rain hit him in the face. The metal stairs were slippery, occasionally letting out squeaks and squawks, as if the steel structure itself were threatening to fall into pieces any minute, which made John nervous. The building's elevator hadn't functioned since God knows when, so he had no choice but to climb up the damned stairs. Getting smashed with the lousy staircase like a piece of garbage wasn't high on his to-do list, so he ran up the stairs.

As an actor, he went to the gym to do occasional workouts and training, but that didn't mean he was a big fan of vigorous exercise. On normal days, he would have shied away from walking up the rusty metal stairs of a sad-looking apartment. Actually, he wouldn't have set a foot in this neighborhood unless he was starring in a gangster movie or TV show, hopefully as the lead role. After all, it wasn't the area where any of the characters of *Sex and the City* lived. It almost felt comical that this neighborhood was still included in Manhattan.

While he mentally dissed Washington Heights, he completely forgot about his own social status as one of the least important actors in off-Broadway theater scenes. He also conveniently forgot the fact that, if it weren't for the tiny apartment in Brooklyn, which he inherited from a late great-aunt, and financial assistance provided by Ruth, he couldn't even keep a roof over his head.

He jumped and let out a girly yelp when a rat the size of an obese Chihuahua ran up the stairs from behind and went ahead of him.

"What kind of miserable excuse of an unknown artist lives here?" he muttered to himself after some cussing—again, completely forgetting the fact he happened to be one of those miserable excuses himself.

As he approached the third floor where Ivan lived, John remembered his last exchange of words over the phone with his enemy, and being annoyed so greatly that he almost felt like his blood flowed backward.

About thirty minutes ago, he received a strange phone call from Ivan.

Getting a phone call from him was a rare event, mostly because the feeling of hate between the two of them was mutual. Both were Ruth's kept men, and both were trying their best to convince her that the other guy wasn't worth her time—or money.

"Hey, John the loser, I've got bad news for you," Ivan declared as soon as John picked up the call. He sounded like he was drunk, but there was something in his voice that made John nervous.

"What are you talking about?"

"I'm calling to deliver a piece of special news to you. Now that I've acquired something to make me the El Greco of the twenty-first century, you're so out of sight to Ruth and out of the picture. She is going to choose me, and she'll dump you like a piece of garbage. Ha! Why don't you curl up in the corner of your tiny apartment and cry like a little girl?" Then the line went dead.

Immediately, John rushed from his apartment and took a cab to Washington Heights. He was determined to confront the SOB and beat him till he cried like a baby.

As soon as he reached apartment 312, he banged on the door.

"Who's there?" Ivan's voice demanded from inside.

"It's John. Open up."

"No way."

"I have something to say to you. Open up!" John banged on the door even louder.

"Stop bothering me. Just leave!"

"No, I won't. I won't 'just leave' until I get to talk to you face-to-face."

"I have nothing to say to you. You have to leave, or else I'll call the cops and have you—"

It seemed Ivan was about to say "arrested," but his words stopped short.

Instead of menacing words, he let out an agonizing moan. It became louder and escalated to a high-pitched shriek.

Then came silence.

"Hey, Ivan, what's going on?" John askcd as he switched from banging to knocking on the door.

No reply.

"Come on, Ivan. Open up. You can't fool me!" John yelled at the door, but again, no reply.

"Guess what, Ivan? You're all words and no action. You're just running away from me because I'm stronger than you. Ha!" John yelled at the door and turned on his heels to leave. After taking a couple of steps, he went back to his love opponent's door.

"Loser!" Yelling, he jumped and kicked at the door. He was just trying to make his point, but the worn-out door made of a thin veneer wood panel broke easily.

John lost his balance and fell onto the cold concrete corridor.

"Crap," he groaned.

Lying on the hard, cold floor, John was half expecting Ivan to come out of hiding, yelling at him, but no one came from inside. Instead, a twentyish Asian guy stormed out from next door.

"What is the matter with you?" he demanded.

John mumbled an apology and the guy went back to his room.

Something wasn't right.

He got up and reached for the now-broken door. It was locked, but he could put his hand inside to unlock the door.

Getting inside was a piece of cake.

"Hello?" John said. "Ivan? Um… Sorry about the door."

As he opened it, dim light came into his eyes.

"Ivan…?"

There was no one in the room.

"What the hell…?" he muttered.

It was a tiny, one-bedroom, matchbox-sized apartment. In the living room / dining room / workroom was a 30" x 40" painting sitting on an easel. It was nothing fancy. The whole background was painted in an assortment of dark, boring, and depressing colors. The only part that caught his attention was the large blank area in the canvas. It looked as if whatever was portrayed had run out of the canvas and vanished.

He advanced closer to the painting.

On the side of the canvas, the title *G.H.O.U.L.* was written in pencil.

Glancing down, John gasped as he spotted an assortment of men's clothes, including underwear, heaped on the floor, as if someone stripped off those garments and left.

Or whoever had those garments on had disappeared like smoke.

"Hey, Ivan?" Not grasping the situation, John searched the apartment for his rival, but he couldn't find any signs of him.

John glared at the heap of clothes in front of the canvas for a while. Then, out of the blue, he kicked the garments. As the shirt, pants, and underwear scattered, something like pebbles of stone rolled over the floor.

"What the…?" John picked up a piece. It looked like a tooth—small, white, and hard, with a metal bolt on the base.

As an actor, he liked to play the role of a tough guy, but in reality, he wasn't. Startled, he dropped the tooth on the floor. When it hit, he caught a glimpse of several other pieces. Each was about the size of a chick pea, yellowish white with dark brown stains.

The moment he realized the stains might be blood, John passed out and dropped on the hard floor.

CHAPTER 1

Green and purple... Seriously? Who had the deciding vote in determining the color schemes of this hideous building? USCIS? Or FBI? I wondered as I stood in front of 26 Federal Plaza in Manhattan, my new workplace.

It was my first day of work at the FBI's New York Field Office, and I wasn't sure if I was happy or unhappy about my new career as an FBI special assistant.

If this were a book, movie, or TV show, I would be a budding FBI special agent or something really badass.

In that case, I would be ready to protect and defend the United States as I fought menacing terrorists or a group of evil aliens trying to invade Earth. In addition, if it were fiction, I would look like Jennifer Lawrence and have a really flashy educational background under my belt, such as having graduated from an Ivy League school at the top of my class. Not to mention I would be driving a Ferrari or a Lamborghini, or a Mercedes at least.

Unfortunately, none of the above characteristics applied. After all, I was talking about my life, and lately, it kind of sucked.

My name is Amanda Meyer. I'm a twenty-five-year-old American with Italian, English, and a little bit of Romanian heritage.

I'm an American woman in my mid-twenties, but that's all I have in common with *The Hunger Games* star. I stand at 5'4", and I'm a size or two—or maybe three—larger than her dress size.

I don't have an Ivy League education under my belt, mostly because Harvard, Yale, Columbia, and all other such schools rejected my application. As for the car, I don't even own one. I used to drive a relatively new Toyota Camry, but I sold it. I was trying my best to convince myself I didn't need to have a car anymore now that I moved back to my parents' home in Queens, New York.

About a month ago, I was a medical student in North Carolina. I was in my third year—busy studying for exams, memorizing all the medical and surgical knowledge, and doing clinical rotations—until I got kicked out of medical school.

Don't get me wrong. I wasn't a bad student.

So I didn't hold high hopes of graduating at the top of my class, or someday becoming a Nobel laureate. Then again, my academic performance wasn't that bad. I was usually at around the top 50-60 percent of the class. At a place where the majority of your classmates have an IQ of 180 and up, even being a mediocre student took lots and lots of hard work.

Anyway, the odds of my finishing medical school and becoming a doctor or getting some cushy job with some pharma/biotech/insurance company were pretty high. Back then, I used to picture myself in the future driving a nice car and vacationing in beautiful resorts.

Generally speaking, doctors are highly regarded in today's society. Sometimes, people talked about the top-notch physicians in comparison with God. On the other hand, I was held in comparison with the Grim Reaper and the Angel of Death. And as a result, I got kicked out of medical school, saying good-bye to my life plan as a doctor.

Oh, did I mention getting kicked out of

medical school didn't offset my larger-than-life student loan?

So, there I stood, with no degree under my belt and a huge debt up to my eyeballs. To rub salt in the wound, Justin, my now ex-fiancé, had called off our engagement. We went to the same med school. He was two years my senior and was already in his first year of residency training. Obviously, he had assessed the pros and cons of staying with me and concluded that staying with a woman called the Grim Reaper wasn't likely to boost his value as a surgeon.

As I stood in front of the East German-style building, I felt so depressed, I almost started sobbing.

Look at the bright side, Mandy... I tried to convince myself.

At least I was going to have a job, and their offer wasn't bad. I would be able to make monthly payments on my student loan and make a decent living. Maybe I could even move out of my parents' townhouse in a year or so.

Actually, I wasn't eager to take this job when I received the offer, but Mom and Dad insisted I should. They were not very keen on spending the rest of their lives paying off my student loan.

"Miss, you've been standing here for a long time." Frowning, the guy in a guard's uniform gave me an accusing glare.

"Um... I'm sorry. I got a little bit distracted. I'm supposed to start working here today," I said, but based on his deep frown, I was positive he didn't believe me.

"Oh, I'm running late. I've got to go...." I attempted to walk away, but he grabbed my arm.

"What is the purpose of—?" the guard started interrogating me, but he didn't get to finish his sentence.

"Good morning, Stanley," a male voice boomed from behind us. It was a deep, smooth baritone—clear, calm, and confident. Without turning back to see him, I found myself picturing a tall guy with a certain level of sexiness. He continued, "For your information, you don't want to mess with her. Guess what? So far, she's killed three men just by touching them. In addition, it's her first day working as my assistant. If you convince her to leave without even starting the job, Hernandez will be so pissed."

I had a remote knowledge that the head of the FBI's New York Office was named Hernandez.

"Mr. Rowling!" The guard's response sounded more like a surprise than an acknowledgement.

When he straightened himself, he was no longer grabbing my arm, too busy saluting Mr. Rowling.

"I am awfully sorry for my rude behavior. I didn't know she was your new assistant."

Then, turning to me, he apologized profusely. "I'm awfully sorry, ma'am."

If eyes could speak, his were saying, 'Why didn't you mention you worked for *him*?'

"Okay, so we're all cool," said Mr. Rowling.

I turned back to thank and greet him, but words failed me.

He was tall, athletic, and had broad shoulders. He had flawless fair skin and dark hair styled in a conservatively messy 'do. His mesmerizing green eyes looked almost blue, and his cheekbones were prominent. His nose and jaw were sculpted to perfection.

In a nutshell, he was drop-dead gorgeous.

But that wasn't the only reason I was at a loss for words.

"You are the—" Clenching my teeth and fists, I searched for words.

Though I didn't remember his name, I did recognize him, in an 'I am so going to kill him if I ever lay my eyes on him again' way.

"Yeah, I'm Rick Rowling." He flashed his perfect set of pearly whites. Obviously, he didn't read my mind. "Hi, Mandy. Nice meeting you again." He extended his right hand toward me.

I took a deep breath. I had no fucking idea why this guy was so familiar with me to call me by the nickname I'd used since kindergarten. Before today, we had met only once for just a couple of hours, and during that short period of time, he killed my future as a doctor.

I took his hand, half wishing he'd drop dead on the spot.

After all, he was the one who convinced the Chapel Hill Police Department and my medical school that I'm the Grim Reaper.

Book 2: W is for Wicked:
http://amzn.to/29s5SLj

Murder investigation is tricky—especially when the deceased threatens to kill you...

FREE on Kindle Unlimited!

Former medical student turned FBI special assistant Amanda Meyer isn't thrilled about her new gig as a ghost whisperer, especially now that she has the spirit of a departed drag queen following her around.

But having a pal on the other side may just come in handy when a billionaire's widow meets her untimely demise and Amanda and her oh so sexy boss, Rick Rowling, head of the Paranormal Cases Division, are called in to find the killer.

With nine scandalous suspects, nine questionable motives, one dead witness and one cryptic clue, the bureau's dynamic duo should be able to solve this case by the numbers, but the victim's restless soul wants revenge while the clock is ticking. What's the girl nicknamed The Grim Reaper to do? M may be for Murder, but W is for Wicked.

PROLOGUE

"There are some men who enter a woman's life and screw it up forever."
—Janet Evanovich, One for the Money

My name is Stephanie Plum, and for me, the man who takes pleasure in periodically screwing up my life is Joseph Morelli....

No, that's a downright lie—I mean, I'm kidding—for the most part.

I'm not the world's most famous, most popular, or perhaps, the richest female bounty hunter. As for Joseph Morelli, I haven't even met him, much less got screwed by him. Um... don't misunderstand me, I'm talking conceptually, not physically or carnally.

Okay, so I know it's wrong to impersonate a total stranger, but excuse me, you need to cut me some slack.

My life sucks way worse than Stephanie's. Sometimes, I'm oh-so-desperate to fool myself that I have a life somewhere, anywhere but where I'm stuck.

My name is Amanda Meyer. Most of the time, I'm called Mandy, and that's the acceptable part—I can live with this nickname. Like Stephanie, I work in a law enforcement field, except I'm with the FBI instead of a bonds office in New Jersey. Unlike her, I'm not filthy rich. She's described as constantly struggling for money in her books, but I know she's rich.

Okay, so she goes on about how she's stuck with a dead-end job forecasted as mostly cloudy with chances of raining bullets and dead bodies and exploding vehicles, how she ended up selling her electronics, and how little food she's left at home— but that's just her words. On second thought, it's impossible to stay poor when you're the star of a megahit series. She probably has her millions stashed somewhere, such as a private bank in Switzerland. In my previous life, I was anticipating a decent life for my future, if not being obscenely rich. I was going to become a doctor, but that career option is now gone, baby, gone. Thanks to getting booted out of medical school with no degree and a humongous student loan, I'm deep in debt up to my eyeballs.

And, believe me, there actually are some men who pop into a woman's life from out of nowhere— like some kind of a genie, leprechaun, or ghost—with the sole purpose of messing with it.

By the way, did I mention that I have not just one, but two men, hexing my life?

For starters, there's Rick Rowling. He's the head of Paranormal Cases Division at the FBI's New York City field office. He became my boss by practically butchering my medical career before it even started. Standing at 6'2" with lean, hard muscles in all the right places, he's hot, sexy, and comes with intense green eyes. He happens to be the only heir to the huge, multi-billion, security conglomerate USCAB—United States Cover All Bases—which means he's ridiculously rich. Unfortunately, he also happens to be an outrageous, egotistical smartass who'd kill to generate trouble and mayhem just for the sake of his own pastime.

I'm not exaggerating. During the investigation of our first case, we were close to being eaten by a bunch of unperishable, monstrous creatures. So I'm trying my best to keep a good distance from him, but he tends to pop in to dinners with my folks at my parents' home.

And there's another guy, Jackie, also known as Jackson Frederick Orchard, who was a budding Broadway actor.

It all happened last November when Rowling and I were walking Pier 26 in Tribeca, where I saw something—no, *someone*—who should be absolutely discernible…

"Cool!" Rick Rowling grinned while walking in the same park where we met Jackie the day before.

"I know! It's totally fab!" Jackie agreed contently.

They were acting like a couple of nine-year-old boys admiring a new toy. Except, their focus wasn't on a new Xbox or hoverboard that actually lets you float and fly in the air. Also, technically, the two of them weren't communicating with each other.

Jackie could see and hear Rowling, but things didn't work out the other way around, because Rowling couldn't see or hear Jackie, which meant he couldn't see Jackie's revealing, skintight outfit in neon green and hot pink, the big hair like Shakira, or the snow-white boa headdress. Not that my boss had impaired vision or hearing, though… it's complicated. He couldn't even see the huge necklace spelling 'FESTIVE' hanging from Jackie's neck.

It was sad that Rowling missed so many colorful things in front of his eyes. Still, at the same time, he was lucky, since he didn't see the huge laceration on the side of Jackie's abdomen, or the little portion of intestines peekabooing from the wound. On top of all that, Jackie was acting a little bit too intimate toward Rowling—for example, raining him with kisses, trying to grope his derrière, and so on. Though Jackie's hands always went through Rowling's body instead of actually landing on his private areas, my boss seemed somewhat uncomfortable whenever he was touched on his butt. So, he might have been feeling something....

Anyway, I happened to be the hot topic du jour. To be more precise, my newly discovered ability to interact with Jackie was.

"You know what, Mandy? So far, you've totally nailed it. All the details you mentioned were accurate. You even correctly described the parts yet to be disclosed to the media, which means you're actually communicating with Jackie. Holy crap, you're phenomenal!" Rick Rowling announced enthusiastically. "By utilizing your new skill, our case closure rate's guaranteed to hit a new high."

"Well, I don't know...," I mumbled in uncertainty. I glanced at Jackie, who was standing by my side. "Maybe he's the only dead person I can communicate with, or maybe—" *He might be my imagination, illusion, or hallucination*

"Okay, Mandy. Relax." Rowling reached for my shoulder, but before his hand touched me, Jackie butted in between us.

"So, Mandy, are you ready to find the SOB who stabbed me to death? Now that I have shared all the juicy details about my case with you," Jackie, who turned into a ghost after getting murdered, said expectantly.

Yeah, you heard me right. I said Jackie is a ghost. Actually, he's not one of those common, boring ghosts, because he's a ghost of a drag queen, and he's urging me to help catch his killer.

"Of course, I know you're ready to kick ass,

considering you've got this hottie hunk FBI agent as a partner. No offence, but I'd love to team up with him without you between us as a translator, and it'd be way nicer if only I could touch him." The ghost of a drag queen chattered nonstop. "By the way, I told you that I preferred to be referred to as *she*, not *he*. I might be a super actor who can be anybody, but I'm a girl at heart." Jackie had the audacity to make tsk-tsk sounds and correct me.

"Um… sorry about that," I mumbled in apology, thinking, *Seriously? A girl at heart? A diva to the bone sounds way more accurate.*

Meanwhile, Jackie went on. "By the way, Mandy, don't even think about pretending you don't see me. You can try shutting your eyes and covering your ears, but you just can't ditch me like old undergarments infesting your closet. I have waited for three years, for Pete's sake! If you abandon me, I'll haunt you like the devil till you go totally cuckoo yourself."

As he—no, *she*—threatened me, the gut peeking out of the wound seemed to be vibrating, as if it represented his—not his, *her*—anger.

Man, she sounds serious… "Oh, no, Jackie, I've never thought about abandoning you!" I flashed a reassuring smile, but inside I wanted to scream and run away. Deep in my mind, I was skeptical about Jackie—like if she *really* exists—and I wanted to state my skepticism loud and clear. But at the same time, if I was a ghost of a murder victim and someone who can hear my voice treats me like I don't exist, I'd be devastated—as if I got murdered not just once but twice. Also, it wouldn't be pretty if the ghost kept to her promise of haunting me like hell. Gosh, I needed a psychiatrist… or a drink strong enough to knock me down unconscious.

"Good." She nodded.

At this time, I knew the chances of the ghost diva departing to a better place like most dead people were practically nonexistent.

"And think of the cool prospects, Mandy." While I was being threatened by Jackie, Rowling's hand had already gone through Jackie and was patting my shoulder. "We can interview dead politicians and high-profile bureaucrats, make them spill their guts, and put our hands on dirty little secrets of our highest-ranking personnel—such as the President of the United States."

"E-excuse me? We? Did you just say *we*?" I stuttered.

"Hmm, that sounds good," Jackie chimed in. "Grasping the VIP's dirty secrets is always good because you can use them as leverage."

"Yeah, it's awesome!" Rowling beamed. "We can practically control the government by utilizing the intel obtained from dead people. Can it get any better?"

I took a deep breath and looked my boss in the eye. "Excuse me, Rick. You told me you can't see or hear Jackie, right?"

"Yup." His intensely deep green eyes looked straight back at me. "Why do you ask that?"

"Hey, Mandy, is there any chance he's gay?" Jackie interjected, trying without success to pick up a lock of brown hair hanging over Rowling's forehead. Before I answered, she continued. "No, he's not gay. I can tell. I can just tell. Assuming he's a straight guy, shouldn't he be swatting me like a bug when I'm getting a little bit too intimate with him? You're so skeptical, Mandy. He's telling you the truth. There is no way he can see or hear me. I recommend you stop doubting. Joy and happiness will run away from you if you keep on taking a dim view of everything."

She had a point. Considering they weren't channeling with each other, I was stuck not only with Rick Rowling but also with Jackie the ghost, who was as outrageous as Rowling.

"Oh, I found another reason to conclude that he can't see me." Jackie went on. "If he's gay or bi, he should be cooing whenever I touch him, shouldn't he?"

Slapping my forehead, I groaned.

"What's up, Mandy?" Rowling and Jackie said in unison as if they had no clue why I looked so grim.

"Never mind," I said, wishing it were just a weird, wicked dream and not my life, or my career....

* * *

Once being born to this world, every life is destined to die—eventually, sooner or later, and at least once. Everybody knows that, but most people do not expect people close to them to suddenly go cold, motionless, and totally uncommunicative, as in a deathly silence, especially when they had no existing serious health problems.

"Holy smoke!"

When Marcus heard those words in Willow's high-pitched voice, he nervously twitched his impeccably trimmed and manicured eyebrows.

It was the moment he heard the telltale *thud!* He was almost certain that the maid had committed another faux pas—like dropping a heavy object, or falling a few steps down the grand staircase—without seeing it for himself, because he had witnessed Willow flopping more often than he wished to see.

Marcus looked at the clock. It was just a few minutes to 9:00 p.m. He couldn't help wondering why the maid had to make another blunder just minutes before finishing her shift and leaving. He sighed, thinking that Willow wouldn't be happy to help fix whatever mess she had created. But when her next wail came saying, *"Madame... Madame! Are you all right?"* he could no longer sit quietly in his waiting room.

As soon as he burst into the foyer, he demanded, "What is the matter, Willow?"

"Oh... Mr. Marcus, I'm so glad you're here!" the maid said breathlessly, without standing.

"Are you—" Marcus started to ask, but then gasped. "Oh my goodness, Madame Giselle!"

To his horror, it was Giselle Carolynn Axtell McCambridge, the head of the McCambridge family, and his very own employer, who was helplessly lying over the bottom steps of the grand staircase. She was bleeding from her head, and the blood was oozing over the white marble step.

Rushing to her side, Marcus inquired, "Madame Giselle? Madame Giselle! Please wake up."

By his side, Willow shrieked, "Madame Giselle!"

"Come on, Willow! Stop shrieking and give me the phone! Now, go and open the gate to secure the access for the ambulance, and notify Mr. Wilfred and Mrs. Wilma-Diane." As Marcus, the butler of the McCambridge mansion, shushed away the maid, Giselle let out a low groan.

"Madame Giselle! Are you all right? Are you hurting?" As soon as he finished speaking to the 911 operator, he peppered his employer with questions.

"Marcus…" twitching her delicate eyebrows, Giselle whispered in her usual commanding voice. "You don't need to scream at me. I haven't gone deaf." Then she grimaced. "Ow… it's so painful!"

Her voice was strong, and her pale gray eyes were piercing as always, but obviously, she was in pain.

"Madame, the ambulance is on the way. Please relax and rest assured—"

"Ambulance? Did I just hear that I'd be riding an ambulance? How embarrassing!" Touching her head, Giselle frowned. "No McCambridge has ever ridden an ambulance."

"Which means you're the very first McCambridge given the honor," Marcus responded, forcing himself to display some humor and a reassuring smile.

"By the way, Marcus," Giselle said, looking at her now bloodstained fingertips, "you need to call the police as well, because someone pushed me off the stairs."

"Oh, my…" The butler gasped, but soon regained his composure. "Who committed such dreadfulness?"

"Marcus, will you collaborate with the police to catch the culprit?" Giselle reached for the butler.

Taking the mistress's hand, Marcus consoled her. "Madame Giselle, you will soon feel better. The doctors at Beth Israel will make sure you'll be as good as…" He stopped talking when he realized Giselle was writing the letter W on his palm in blood—over and over. "Madame Giselle?"

He intended to ask her for the meaning of *W*.

"It is by no means acceptable to push someone off the stairs." Before Marcus spoke, Giselle did, looking the butler straight in his eyes. "Marcus, I recall that you like Jeeves, am I correct?"

"Yes, Madame. You are correct. I'm a huge fan of Jeeves." Even though Marcus was dying to ask more about *W*, he knew his mistress too well to butt in. When Giselle McCambridge had something to say, she had to say it, and there was no room for the butler to change the subject.

"Good. Make sure that this crooked criminal who hurt me gets caught and justice is served. Be my Jeeves."

"I will, Madame Giselle. I will be your Jeeves. By the way, who is *W*?"

"*W* is... I mean... find..." As Giselle started to talk, she grimaced and gasped for air. Her entire body convulsed for a moment. Then she closed her eyes, never to open them again.

Find *W*—these were the last words of Giselle Carolynn Axtell McCambridge.

By the time the family members and the visitors came to see what the commotion was about, Giselle had become unresponsive.

The paramedics arrived and took her to Beth Israel, but even the world's greatest physicians couldn't bring her back to life.

Giselle's death was a total shock to Marcus. Considering her advanced age—seventy-seven, that was, though she stopped counting since hitting fifty—Giselle was extremely healthy, and her death was unexpected. At the same time, Marcus knew that solving the assault, which was upgraded to a murder, of Giselle McCambridge had become the last mission assigned by his employer for the past twenty-five years. By filling the blanks and reading between the lines of his previous conversation with his employer, he knew that *W* was the culprit.

Under normal circumstances, the most straightforward answer would be someone with names starting with W. And considering that there was no burglar at McCambridge mansion at the time of the crime, it was only natural to assume that whoever committed this crime would be someone at the house.

The only problem was everyone at the McCambridge mansion at the time of the crime had at least one W as the initial of their names—including Marcus Warne-Smith himself.

Book 3: Wicked Little Secret:
http://amzn.to/2du4JWy

Everyone has secrets--ghosts are no exception...

FREE on Kindle Unlimited!

Finding her body taken over by a ghost with unfinished business while entertaining a tempting (yet dangerous sounding) invitation from Rick Rowling-- her boss--has Amanda Meyer, FBI special assistant and resident ghost whisperer for the Paranormal Cases Division, in a tailspin. Her drag-queen-guardian ghost is acting even stranger than usual, a murder victim holds a clue to finding a stolen sculpture, and a parade of well-meaning family members might just set another murder in motion.

What's the girl nicknamed Grim Reaper to do when a departed witness won't fess up, and she finds herself living with her crazy, arrogant, yet irresistibly sexy boss? Everyone's got secrets, but only the ghosts know whose will be revealed in this hilariously wicked romp in the Paranormal in Manhattan Mystery Series.

Wicked Little Secret is part of the Paranormal in Manhattan Mystery series. If you like fast-paced mysteries full of quirky characters and unexpected twists, you're gonna love *Wicked Little Secret*.

Buy *Wicked Little Secret* and start solving your next mystery today!

Paranormal in Manhattan Mystery Series
Each book in the series is a stand-alone story, but

your enjoyment of each story will be increased if you read them all.

Excerpts:

"By the way, are there any rooms off-limits to me?"

"No. Why?" he said, frowning.

"Well, this place reminds me of Christian Grey's penthouse, so I assumed maybe you have something you'd like to hide from me—such as a torture room."

It was supposed to be a joke, but Rick sucked in air. "How did you know that? Actually, I've got seven of them in the upstairs. Each room has uniquely themed décor and equipment for you know what."

"What?" My eyes widened. It was my turn to gasp for air. "Not just one but seven torture rooms?"

"Yup, so I can shift them every day of the week. I'm sure you'll like them." He winked and ran his finger across my lips. "Don't tell anyone, it's my dirty little secret that I have those rooms."

I opened my mouth to say something, but words failed to come, so I nodded like a bobble-head.

"Good girl." Glancing at his splinted and heavily bandaged right leg, he said casually, "The stairs are a bitch to climb up and down on crutches, so I'd appreciate it if you'd bring down the handcuffs and whips, along with a silk blindfold and hogtie. Oh, I've got a can of whipped cream in the fridge. We'll have tons of fun." He winked.

PROLOGUE

Aurora Westwood was irritable.

As the most celebrated psychic in America, she had it all—bestseller books, her own TV show, a large mansion with a green garden in the Upper West Side, an even larger mansion in the Hamptons, and a smorgasbord of prime-location estates all over the world.

She regarded herself as more of a sorceress than a psychic. The only reason she used the title of psychic was because it had a more captivating effect on American consumers than the term sorceress. She could communicate with and exorcise dead people's spirits, but she also had power to control, manipulate, enslave them, and create magic agents out of lifeless objects.

She saw many imitators emerging into the spotlight and then disappearing throughout her decades-long career. Seeing recycled versions of herself being wiped out of the picture only augmented her confidence. Sometimes, she went so far as to sponsor her imitators secretly, using shell companies, only to dump them later by blowing their cover, revealing their fraudulent nature, and boosting her own reputation.

An earlier incident had upset Aurora. She found a woman as good as herself, maybe even better. This woman, Amanda Meyer was able to disable Aurora's spell without using magical words or anything. She practically broke Aurora's sorcery just by being there. She was working with the FBI, and she didn't seem to be interested in the showbiz industry. However, the woman was much younger than her.

On that fateful day about two months ago, Aurora was scheduled to interview a billionaire's wife—a possible murder victim—in her TV show, *The Voice from the Other End.* In her long career as a psychic medium, Aurora had assisted law enforcement and solved numberless cases, and that day was supposed to turn out to be as glorious as ever. The cameras… TV crews… the setting… everything had been carefully planned and executed for shooting. The episode was promised to be another success, but the FBI and Amanda happened. The case was closed without Aurora's involvement.

Aurora had been surveying and manipulating the entire event using a magic agent disguised as a rosary, but somehow she couldn't take a full control of the whole situation. And she blamed that for Amanda's presence. The rosary had sufficient power to manipulate everyone including the police and the FBI, but the people gathered in place were least affected. Witnessing her spell broken was the last straw for her. The moment Amanda approached and looked at the rosary, it exposed its ugly true form of a magic agent spider. Amanda's power was so strong that the spider, which was originally the size of a rat, had to dissolve into thousands of tiny spiders, to escape from her.

To Aurora's annoyance, she saw a vision of Amanda becoming an obstacle in the near future. It plagued her the entire way from the Midtown TV studio to her home overlooking the Hudson River. Even after taking a long bath, the foreboding image of the newbie psychic remained in her soul.

Sitting at the makeup table in the bedroom, looking into the mirror, she was deep in thought, muttering to herself, "I have to do something about her."

"I know!" All of a sudden, a furry black spider the size of a Chihuahua popped up on the makeup table. "It's about that girl called Mandy, isn't it?" the spider said in a chipper tone.

Without a word, Aurora lifted an arm to swat the monster spider, but she stopped short. The spider wasn't real, for it was a magic agent she had previously created to pass the time. The funny thing was that she had disabled him, but he reappeared in front of her. Also, he was larger than before. The last time they'd talked, the spider was only as large as a rat.

"Don't hit me! I have an idea," the spider said proudly, jumping up and down.

"What idea?" Aurora asked. She detested this creature and its disgusting spider form, but at the same time, she was a little curious about him. "Tell it now, or I'll make you disappear. This time, you're going to perish into total nothingness."

"Wow, I'm scared. Though if I were you, I wouldn't kill me because I'm a part of you, and getting rid of me is synonymous with murdering a part of you." The spider chuckled, but he stopped doing so when Aurora clenched her fist. "Okay, so you're concerned about this Mandy. You want to get her out of the picture before she gets in your way, right?"

"I'm too good for her to get in my way." Aurora shrugged. "Still, she's offensive."

"I know!" the spider enthusiastically agreed. "My guess is that she'll be interviewing many spirits of the dead, won't she?"

"I think so. She's with the feds… aha!" A

wide smile spread across Aurora's face. "I can use the help of those spirits! Especially if I provide them with a little portion of my power. After all, the kind of spirits the feds would need help with will be obsessed with wrath and vengeance. Yes, I can do it. Definitely!"

With the heavy cloud of irritation clearing from her mind, she felt youthful. She was determined to strike Amanda Meyer out of the picture.

CHAPTER 1

The Manhattan skyline outside the office windows was uncharacteristically clean and translucent—radiant, even. The rain and thunderstorm that poured and roared until half an hour ago had washed away all the grime and dirt from the air. I was glad for that because I was expecting to go out soon, and I appreciated the nice weather. The rain had started just minutes before I made it back to the office from my lunch break, and I didn't enjoy my previous run in the drizzle.

It was the moment when I took a look at my phone, computer screen, and the clock on the wall for the umpteenth time that Rick Rowling made a comment. "Mandy, you've been checking the time every thirty seconds for the past hour. Why don't you just set an alarm on your phone?"

"I know, but even if I used an alarm, I'd have to keep checking the time. I really don't want to be late for this appointment." I glanced at the clock again. I was a little nervous because it was the first time I'd be working on my own and collaborating with people from another department. No, a little nervous was an understatement. Actually, nerves were somersaulting in my stomach. "I want to make a good impression," I admitted. At the very least, I wanted to be remembered as a punctual person.

"You can show off your skills, but don't act like you'd give anything to please them. If you give them the wrong impression, they'll start taking advantage of you. Don't ever short-sell yourself, because that means short-selling me as well. I don't want that to happen. Okay?" Rowling warned me. My boss hated to be exploited, mostly because he was the one who usually took advantage of others.

"Okay. I got it." I nodded, making a mental note not to be underrated by the people I was going to work with.

My name is Amanda Meyer, but most people call me Mandy. I happen to work for the FBI's New York City field office. If it was a book, film, or TV show, I would be a special agent, profiler, or sniper serving our country and protecting the citizens from terrorists and other catastrophes, such as vicious attacks by deranged, psychopathic aliens. But I'm talking about my life, and it's not as exciting or glamorous as those of fictional characters from the big screens or the actresses portraying these characters.

My job title is special assistant, though I haven't figured out what is so *special* about being an assistant. Perhaps it's just the feds' jargon of calling common things special so they sound distinctive, or it might be that they're simply obsessed with specialness to the point of naming positions at the in-bureau cafeteria as special cook, special barista, and special cashier.

As a special assistant, most of my tasks were clerical, such as keeping case files up to date, answering phone calls, calendar creation and maintenance, and making coffee for my wacky, temperamental boss. Oh, I forgot to include "communication with dead people" in the list of my job duties—or maybe I had deliberately omitted that task.

Yes, you heard me right, I talk to dead people. On this particular day, I was going to interview a murdered IT engineer in order to help agents from the counterterror unit obtain information from the victim.

I know. In general, we don't interview dead people, mostly because they don't talk to us. Asking the people in Deadville how they ended up dying, and who killed them was considered a special asset. Presumably because I happened to be a part of the Paranormal Cases Division, which dealt with cases involving supernatural elements, and I was the only person at the New York City field office with the ability to communicate with the deceased.

Anyway, my ghost whisperer skill just popped up out of nowhere since I started this job. And guess what? It's not easy, especially when the interviewee is either unaware of his/her death, vengeful, or has pathological liar traits. Things can get ugly, stressful, and downright weird sometimes. I once tried to quit talking to dead people and focus on clerical tasks, but Sheldon Hernandez, the head of the New York City field office, dismissed my plea immediately.

I suppose that I should be grateful for my good fortune. At least my name isn't Clarice Starling and I don't have to deal with Hannibal the Cannibal. So far, Rick Rowling is my only colleague in the Paranormal Cases Division. He's monikered as Zombie Repellant. Not that he smells of rotten flesh or looks like an undead. Just the opposite actually, he's exceptionally good-looking. Perhaps even better-looking than your average heartthrobs on the big screens, and he smells wonderful...sexy, even. This unearthly nickname has more to do with his outrageous, loose-cannon attitude. But at least I haven't caught him cracking open any human skulls and eating their brains.

PI Assistant Extraordinaire Mysteries:
Book 1: Ghostly Murder: http://amzn.to/204aWJ4

A murder in a locked room…
A faceless ghost…
Throw in a cross-dressing detective-savant plus his
assistant extraordinaire in this new mystery series!

A high profile murder calls for a high profile detective.

When the famous Sushi Czar is found dead in a room that's locked from the inside, the evidence just doesn't add up. Of course a killer ghost (supernatural killer) is no match for the deductive skills of Michael Archangel. The fabulous cross-dressing former FBI agent can rock a set of sky high stilettos and assemble clues like puzzle pieces, but can he actually prove a ghost committed murder?

Only his assistant knows for sure. Former housewife and London socialite Kelly Kinki (it's Kinki ending with an I not a Y) may someday be the Watson to Archangel's Holmes, but for now, she's following orders, coveting his fashion sense and learning from the master PI that there's something truly fishy about this case.

CHAPTER 1

There's a first time for everything.

I was walking in the forest all by myself. It was a sunny day in late March, but in the shadows of tall trees, it was dark, cold, and creepy. Also, having a group of crows—a.k.a. a *murder* of crows—squawking over my head did nothing to calm my nerves.

Don't get me wrong. I was not an adventurer wannabe or a plant hunter wandering about some exotic forest in the middle of nowhere with a totally unpronounceable name, such as *Tweebuffelsmeteenskootmorsdoodgeskietfontein* in Africa. On the contrary, I was one of those so-called city workers. My job title was the personal assistant to a certain private investigator based in McLean, Virginia.

I was in Arlington, the 'good' suburb of Washington DC. Though there was a metro station in walking distance, this part of the town was very quiet, giving it the feel of a godforsaken land. I wasn't exaggerating. Maybe the fact that a man's dead body was found nearby had something to do with my perception. In addition, considering he was stabbed to death, this neighborhood might not be such a good area. Oh, did I mention there was some wacko serial rapist still running loose in the neighborhood? As a woman with no expertise in martial arts, I had a gazillion reasons to be spooked.

Walking in the forest wasn't something I was

doing by choice. Michael Archangel, my eccentric employer with a diva personality, made me do so. My mission was to look for either pantyhose, a ski mask, or big granny panties. Any of those items were supposed to help my employer with his most recent case, but I couldn't figure out why or how. Anyway, I had never dreamed about going treasure-hunting for potentially used undergarments in the urban forest at the age of twenty-nine.

When I was a kid, I wanted to be an alchemist or a doctor. But the reality wasn't rosy enough to realize either of my childhood dreams. First of all, there was no alchemist school. In addition, my test score wasn't good enough for premed programs. So my mom and fifth—or was it sixth?—faux-dad sent me to a finishing school in Switzerland where I mastered the art of eating an orange using a knife and a fork. After that, I became a housewife in London, obtained a bachelor's degree in art, and then I got a divorce. People in Europe, especially rich people in London, still called me 'the bitch who used to be married to that swindler' a.k.a. the man who had committed the largest investment scam in the history of Great Britain.

Here's my point: Education is so overrated.

My name is Kelly Kinki. Yes, it's my real name as written on my birth certificate. No, my surname is not a joke. And no, I'm not into kinky sex. Kinky or otherwise, it had been a while since I had sex.

As I thought about sex, I realized how much I hated walking through the creepy woods. I could think of much better things to do—such as tackling crossword puzzles or building a robot vacuum cleaner from scratch—but sometimes, you had to do what you had to do.

All of the sudden, one of the crows let out an especially menacing squawk as something started chirping and vibrating at the same time, startling me.

"Holy crap!"

A second later, I realized it was coming from my purse and reached for my phone.

"Hello? What can I do for you, Mr. Archangel?" I said to the person on the other end, who happened to be the one responsible for my current situation.

There was no response.

"Hello? Mr. Archangel?"

Still nothing.

From the other end, I could hear muffled voices. I recalled a bunch of retired gentlemen, who resided in the neighborhood, gathering at the crime scene. When I left there, they were busy gossiping. In my mind's eyes, I could almost see and hear them cracking jokes and laughing their *as*—I mean, laughing their *pants* off. A moment later, I finally got a whispered response from Archangel.

"Password."

"What? Password? What are you talking about?" I said, puzzled.

"You need to provide the password of Michael Archangel Investigations."

"Excuse me? I've got your name on my caller ID. And it's my voice. You can recognize me from my voice, can't you?"

"No. You sound different," he said. "Actually, you sound pretty much annoyed."

"Come on, so I'm pretty much annoyed right now, but still, it's me. Besides that, you're the one who's calling my phone, so you should know—" I was tempted to go on with my rant, but I realized it was easier to just tell the password.

"All right! I'll tell the password." Then I stopped short. What was the password? I knitted my eyebrows. It was something about artists. Oh yeah—Matisse, Bonnard, and Rothko—that was it.

"Matisse, Bonnard," I said my part and waited for him to say "Rothko" but—

"Okay, let's get to the point."

"Hey!" I protested. "You're supposed to finish the password before getting to the point. I said 'Matisse, Bonnard' and you're supposed to say 'Rothko.' Without your finishing, the password isn't complete!"

"What are you babbling, Kelly? It's me, Michael Archangel. You should be able to recognize me from my voice. Otherwise, you must be affected with an early-onset of Alzheimer's."

All right, he had a point. The password was pretty much worthless since I knew I was talking to Archangel. His voice was deep, husky, and somewhat seductive, per usual. In addition, I knew no one else as fuc—I mean, *freaking* annoying as him.

"So, what's up, Mr. Archangel? Any progress?"

"Yeah. The cops found the item I was looking for. I knew it was somewhere in the ground. Anyway, you can come back to the tennis court."

"What? So you sent me to this creepy forest fully knowing I wouldn't be the one to find the granny panties?"

"Actually, the discovered item turned out to be a ghost mask."

"That's not the point. You sent me, of all people, to go into this deep, spooky, and potentially dangerous forest for a wild goose chase of a ghost mask you didn't even bother to mention in the first place. On top of it all, I'm talking about these woods located near the site where a twenty-four-year-old female office worker was nearly raped last night for Pete's sake!" I spat.

I knew about her because, this morning, local news was all about this serial rapist in Arlington. In the past month, at least five women had been brutally raped. I was more than concerned about my own safety.

"Good thing you're much older than twenty-four years old," was Archangel's reply.

"Excuse me? That's not the point." I continued. "This rapist has not yet been ID'd, much less arrested. Has it ever come to your mind that the rapist is still hiding in the darkness of these woods, determined to assault another young, innocent, and defenseless woman, such as your assistant? Imagine it. I might become his next prey. Aren't you worried about me?"

Without responding to my bullets of questions, he said, "Come back to the tennis court pronto. If you don't come back before I finish wrapping up the case, I'll leave without you."

And the line went dead.

Words like *manners* and *protocol* must be missing from my employer's dictionary.

Man, I really, *really* hated this job.

Book 2: Immortal Eyes: http://amzn.to/1T4DKC3

Serial murder with a sick ritual...
The most unusual way to use Eggs Benedict...
The mismatched duo's race against time...
Former London socialite Kelly Kinki doesn't always see eye to eye with her sexy-as-hell boss Michael Archangel, but she'll follow the brilliant, cross-dressing detective anywhere to help solve their latest case.

Kelly was happy to lay her rep as the Dragon Lady to rest when she moved across the pond, but to catch an eyeball snatching serial killer she'll have to put her skills at fire breathing to the test once again.

A gruesome autopsy, a visit with her ex, and a shocking encounter with a killer compete for craziest day on the job, but nothing can hold a candle to a glimpse of her boss in the buff.

Can Kelly and Archangel solve the case? The ayes have it. PI's that is.

Chapter 1

There's a first time for everything.

I was at a medical examiner's office in rural Virginia. It was my first visit to this place and, actually, it also happened to be my very first trip to a morgue. I was there to attend the autopsy of a woman who allegedly had fallen victim to a brutal murder. So far, I'd seen more than my share of corpses in the past four months; however, I usually saw them at crime scenes and not morgues.

I didn't know much about the statistics of murders, but I had seen lots of homicide victims since starting this job. In the beginning, I kept track of the body count, but I stopped counting after hitting ten on the third day of my current employment. Later, I learned it was just a temporary thing—one of those crazy, busy times—the "on-season" of killing. Anyway, who knew murders had on-seasons? And I'm not talking about Walmart jobs during the holiday season or the wedding industry in June.

My name is Kelly Kinki. Yes, it's my real name as written on my birth certificate. No, I'm not into kinky sex, and no, I'm not making this surname thing up. I'm twenty-nine years old, half Italian-English American and half Japanese. Currently, I'm divorced with no intention or anticipation of a new romantic relationship, much less marriage.

Been there, done that. No thank you very much.

Right then, my mind was completely centered on my career. And guess what, thinking about myself as a super-cool, classy, and oh-so-savvy sleuth—the assistant extraordinaire, to be precise—totally made me happy. The hard bench chair I sat on was no Cassina, and with the faded grayish-green color scheme, sad taste in décor—or lack thereof—and chilly yet stale air, the morgue's waiting room was depressing at the best of times. But I was optimistic. In fact, I was feeling kind of flamboyant because I really, *really* liked the idea of visiting the morgue in line of my job. First of all, I loved the *CSI* TV series, and the prospect of seeing a live autopsy was totally thrilling. Besides that, it was not like the morgues were open to the public so that anybody could take a sightseeing tour and attend an autopsy, right? Having access to this facility was a real privilege.

In my mind, I was picturing myself as a female version of Dr. John Watson, only less geeky. Maybe by taking a part in the autopsy, I might come up with something that could lead to a breakthrough—just like super-assistants of brilliant detectives in fictions do all the time. Maybe I could even kick some ass like a badass assistant, too. In my opinion, it was often the assistant extraordinaire who should get the credit for disentangling the mystery before his/her boss did.

Something warm and fuzzy started to bubble up in my stomach. It wasn't the aftereffect of a lunch burrito. I had to use a great amount of self-restraint to keep myself from singing, *"For the first time in forever, I'll be watching an autopsy!"* like a certain Princess of Arendelle.

I didn't realize I was smiling until I heard, "Why don't you stop grinning like an idiot?" in a deep, husky voice, which belonged to Michael Archangel, the private investigator I worked for, who was sitting next to me on the same bench.

How I managed to forget his presence, I didn't know. If nothing else, the delicate yet distinct scent of Higher Energy by Dior, his fragrance de jour, should have alerted me to his presence.

No thanks to his voice, I was snapped back to the reality that it was him who had access to the morgue, not me. I hadn't clarified with the morgue, but considering I had no authority or qualification, they wouldn't have granted me permission to attend the autopsy if I went there all by myself. I also realized a *real* badass woman wouldn't imagine singing like a Disney Princess while sitting in the morgue's waiting room. The truth was, I wasn't very sure if I *wanted* to attend the autopsy at all.

I was no Dr. Watson. I had no background in medicine. The closest experience I'd ever had with this particular field was having a pediatrician and an orthopedic surgeon as ex-faux-dads. It was the first time for me to see a cadaver getting cut open. The corpses I had seen often had a hole or two, but I had never seen the human innards peekabooing from inside of the body cavity, saying something like "Yoo-hoo?"

As I anticipated this new experience, a gazillion butterflies went wild in my stomach. Okay, so the earlier flamboyance and faux-hardboiled tone were only parts of my façade to hide my nervousness. And speaking of body contents, I wasn't sure if I'd be able to keep my lunch burrito where it belonged.

Discreetly, I took a deep breath to calm my nerves and regain my composure. "I didn't realize you were watching every step of mine, but thanks for your keen attention anyway. I'm flattered," I said nonchalantly.

"Ha." With a snort, Archangel's candy-apple-colored lips curled into a sarcastic smirk. "Don't get me wrong; it's hard to miss someone sitting by my side babbling silly things with goofy grin pasted on her face, especially when this special someone starts drooling."

I felt around my lips with my fingertips, only to find the area completely drool-free.

"I wasn't drooling. You tricked me!" I narrowed my eyes.

"It's because you're such a good comic relief to poke fun at, Kelly," he had the audacity to admit. "But look on the bright side. It was just a joke and not a con. Hey, speaking of a con, did I mention I in no compare to the lying, cheating, jilting, swindling, oh-so-disturbing excuse for a human douchebag who happens to be your ex-husband?" With a lighthearted chuckle, he added, "No pun intended."

Biting my lip, I toyed with the idea of kicking him really hard in the shin. This cra...I mean, *nonsense*, of him dissing Warren and my past marriage was just getting old, and it was oh-so-tempting to finally make a point. But I thought better of it. First off, kicking your employer runs a potentially hazardous risk for your job security. Secondly, most of his words were accurate, especially the part about my ex being a con—as in being a convicted conman. I didn't want to reinforce his cocksureness by getting upset. That would only tip him off that yours truly, indeed, had *feelings* for my ex-husband.

So instead of kicking him, I retorted, "I never drool!"

"Hey, Kelly." Flashing the perfect set of pearly whites, Archangel nudged my elbow. "Look what you've done to her." I followed his gaze and spotted the female receptionist. She was practically gaping at us from behind the counter. My eyes met with hers. I tried a polite, social smile that implied I was not her enemy. She averted her gaze.

"See?" He cocked his head. "You've managed to creep her out in five minutes. What a shame. Now I'm labeled as a PI who's stuck with a weird assistant from La-La Land. Come on, I've got a reputation to maintain." As he shook his head, shining locks of his long, auburn hair swayed like dancing waves.

"I see, so you've got a reputation to maintain." Rephrasing his words, I gave him an up-and-down look. His attire consisted of a skintight, above-the-knee-length dress in vivid magenta and purple fishnet stockings paired with fuck-me-if-you-can high heels. Okay, so the colorful attire flattered his alabaster complexion and the totally gorgeous hair that went midway down his back. Even the heavy makeup wasn't laughable.

Yes, you heard me right. I said he was dressed like a woman. I'm not making any of this up. His outfit de jour was described as skimpy and eye-catching, at best. It was not his Halloween costume on an account that it was early April, not the last day of October. Did I mention that cross-dressing was his "casual/business" attire? I didn't know and didn't want to know what he wore for black-tie events.

I glanced back at the receptionist, who was shaking her head as if trying to clear away the many thoughts running through her mind. I suspected she was taken aback—no, that would be an understatement. I wouldn't be surprised if her brain was caught in a temporary cerebral arrest. Archangel had that effect for many people. Basically, unlike L.A. or Miami, seeing a transvestite in rural Virginia was a very rare occasion, which alone counted as an element of surprise. There was another major element called confusion. Indeed, to the casual eye, his appearance was very confusing. I'm not talking about an esthetically challenged dude playing dress up as a geisha.

He wasn't ugly—lucky him—thanks to inheriting high cheekbones, baby-blue eyes, a well-sculpted nose in a perfect shape that would make Cleopatra cry with envy, and a tall, slender figure from both his mother—Miss California—and grandmother—Miss Greek—he managed to appear almost as strikingly gorgeous as a woman. At least in photos.

Speaking of photos, I supposed perhaps she had seen the pictures of him in the morning paper. Newspapers often carried his photographs. As a Virginia-based PI, he usually consulted with law enforcement, such as the FBI, and worked on tricky, weird, or even the most impossible cases. As a matter of fact, he happened to be a good detective—not just good, but top-notch. He always cracked difficult cases quickly, and as result, newspapers, magazine articles, websites, and sometimes even TV shows reported his accomplishments.

Then again, seeing him in person was a whole different story. Archangel happened to have an even bigger impact in person. He still looked *almost* like a woman. To be precise, he looked more like a supermodel than a woman. I mean, it's not like supermodels look like the rest of us *real* women, right? Those tall, skinny girls are byproducts of women-hating men who dominate the fashion industry and set out to punish us real women by force-feeding us distorted body images, just because we have curves and boobs.

Okay, enough with my little speech. I had mixed feelings about my employer's looks. I know his outfit preference was none of my business, and I believe everyone's entitled to express themselves through fashion. I also appreciated he was the one who caught all the attention, not me. I was the shadow. I enjoyed my invisibility. Then again, it got *a little* awkward when total strangers would stare at us, chattering about 'That totally dazzling supermodel,' and they went on like, 'Who's she? The little one standing next to her? An assistant wannabe? Doesn't she look so mediocre and a little bit heavy?'

And it got *a little* annoying when Archangel caught such chatter and would announce, 'Did you hear that? They think I'm pretty and you're not!'

Did I mention he has a diva personality?

Yeah, it's pretty clear, I ain't no size two. But in my defense, I've got the boobs, uterus, ovaries, and everything a girl needs. Besides that, it's totally rude to judge people based on the physical features for Pete's sake! I might be described as a petite woman, but that doesn't make me *the little one*. I'm the assistant, not a wannabe. Besides that, if you looked carefully, Archangel's jaw was a little bit too strong for a woman and he has an Adam's apple. At 6'3" with lots of toned muscles, what he resembled the most was a Greek Goddess with excessive growth hormone. Or Poseidon in drag.

"Mr. Archangel, why do you think I'm the one who's responsible for spooking her out? Has it ever occurred to you that maybe you're the one who's grabbing her full attention?" I asked.

"Why?" Without answering my question, he arched an eyebrow.

"First of all, she's looking in our direction in general, so both of us are in her sights, and…" I struggled with the words.

"And?" he probed, tapping the backrest of the bench chair with his fingers, which sported nail polish in the same shade of color as the lips.

I was ready to tell him, "And… with all due respect, a giant transvestite is very eye-catching—or rather, an eyesore?" Then it dawned on me that maybe dissing your employer might not be a good move. Call me desperate, but I wasn't made of money and I needed to pay my credit card balance. Unlike Mom, I wasn't a rich-husband-magnet, which meant I really needed to keep my job as a personal assistant to this huge, cross-dressing, brilliant-yet-cynical detective. Maybe I shouldn't have purchased those pricy pillows from Neiman Marcus, but they were so worth it. You want to invest in high-quality pillows to ensure beauty sleep and sweet dreams, especially when you see murdered corpses on a regular basis.

Also, I knew the chances of my scoring other gainful employment anytime soon were practically nonexistent. My resume wasn't something described as highly-decorated. On top of all that, it's not like having lost my last employer in a tragic murder—which wasn't my fault but made me look like a jinx—*and* being an ex-wife of a notorious swindler would catch a potential employer's attention in a good way, would it?

Yes, I was desperate. So much for an independent woman ready to kick ass.

"Kelly? Tell me why you think I'm the one who's creeping her out." Crossing his long legs, Archangel pressed on.

"Well…" With all due respect, I furrowed my

eyebrows like a confused third-grader struggling to grasp the concept of division. "What was I thinking? Isn't it odd that I can't recollect whatever was in my head?"

"Ha. You need to get a head CT to see if you've got a brain at all." Archangel gave a throaty, husky, oh-so-manly laugh. Did I mention his voice was often a dead giveaway for his otherwise confusing gender? When I first met him, I thought he must be gay, but I wasn't so sure any more. I knew his sexual orientation was none of my business, and I respected people with every sexuality, but for a guy who opted to wear women's clothes, Archangel was pretty much lacking delicacy.

Turning my face away from him, I stuck out my tongue. Very mature, I knew. So far, my job duties were one part secretary, one part chauffeur, and one part personal chef. Not to mention being a part-time comic, or rather, laughing stock. Unlike brilliant detectives in literature, Archangel didn't need much assisting when it came to investigation and solving cases. Just like fictional detectives, he was crazy and tended to torment his precious little assistant, having a chuckle at my expense.

I was an assistant extraordinaire who outshone the detective only in my fantasy, and in reality, I was merely a newbie assistant and a butt of jokes to this huge, cross-dressing detective.

It really sucked when the gap between your fancy daydream and the hard, cold, stone-hearted reality was so huge.

Book 3: Deadly Vision: http://amzn.to/1og0Pp9

A sweet n' cold murder…
A newbie, pathetic agent…
And a hot mess…
PI Assistant extraordinaire Kelly Kinki is back, and she's stuck between a hunk and a hard case.
A popular college student has been murdered after visiting a local ice cream shop. The suspect list is short and sweet, but with a fledgling FBI agent tagging along on their investigation, Kelly and her drop dead gorgeous boss Michael Archangel have an extra scoop of trouble.
Trading his dress for a suit and hitting DC's top ten list of eligible bachelors may be business as usual for Archangel, but with a hopeless newbie screwing up the case and Kelly revving up his libido, solving this seemingly ordinary murder might not be cake for America's answer to Sherlock Holmes.

CHAPTER 1

There's a first time for everything.

I was engaged in a tight lip-lock with Michael Archangel, a Virginia-based private investigator and my employer.

There should have been a sequence of events that led to the incident, but I couldn't recall anything at all. And for full disclosure, I was way too preoccupied with the current action to care about how I ended up in a hot kiss with him.

Just like in cartoons, the angel part of me was sitting on my right shoulder, screaming things like "Hello! What's happened to your professionalism? Don't you have anything like work ethics?" And the devil part of me was hooting, jumping, and cheering me from on my other shoulder. "Go, Kelly, go! Think about it, you're not getting any younger!" She was a really naughty devil.

As a professional woman with work ethics and dignity, I didn't listen to the devil and started listening to the angel, and…no, that's a lie. I didn't listen to the angel. Call me an unethical slut, but I was falling for the devil's words.

For a brief moment, our lips parted. I opened my eyes. His baby blues were staring at me so intensely, they seemed a shade or two darker than usual.

He cupped my face in his hands.

"Are you ready?" he whispered. His voice sounded oh-so-sweet on my ears. Then he brushed away my hair and planted a light peck on my forehead.

I mumbled something that meant nothing and

everything. Then I realized he was shirtless and I was only one slutty Agent Provocateur bra and a thong away from…*gulp!* the bedroom.

Breathing hard and admiring his Greek god-like physique, I struggled with his belt buckle, which didn't unbuckle easily. I shivered as Archangel unhooked my bra with just a snap of his fingers.

I closed my eyes. He was reaching south, and then…

* * *

Also, there's a bundle of 3 books available…
Confessions of the Assistant Extraordinaire:
amzn.to/1R3GaO6

Did You Like *Wicked of the Christmas Past*?

Let everyone know by posting a review on Amazon.

When you turn this page you'll be greeted with a request from Amazon to rate this book and post your thoughts on Facebook and Twitter. How cool is that? Be the first one of your friends to use this innovative technology. Your friends get to know what you're reading and I, for one, will be forever grateful to you.

Happy reading!

XOXO, Lotta Smith

48415831R00087

Made in the USA
Middletown, DE
17 September 2017